Should she invite him in?

Would he make a move? Should she make a move?

She stumbled from the truck and grabbed the door. Taking a deep breath, she made a decision and strode toward him.

He met her halfway and took her in his arms before she uttered one word. Wedging a knuckle beneath her chin, he tilted her head back and sealed his lips over hers. The taste of the tiramisu on his mouth made the kiss even sweeter.

If her knees felt weak before, they were positively jelly now. She sagged against him, wrapping her arms around his neck. How would they ever make it inside?

When they finally pulled apart, West said, "I'm sorry. I just couldn't wait any longer."

CAPTURED AT THE COVE

CAROL ERICSON

Harlequin
INTRIGUE

Harlequin® INTRIGUE™

Recycling programs for this product may not exist in your area.

ISBN-13: 978-1-335-45687-8

Captured at the Cove

Copyright © 2024 by Carol Ericson

Harlequin Enterprises ULC
22 Adelaide St. West, 41st Floor
Toronto, Ontario M5H 4E3, Canada
www.Harlequin.com

Printed in Lithuania

MIX
Paper | Supporting responsible forestry
FSC® C021394

Carol Ericson is a bestselling, award-winning author of more than forty books. She has an eerie fascination for true-crime stories, a love of film noir and a weakness for reality TV, all of which fuel her imagination to create her own tales of murder, mayhem and mystery. To find out more about Carol and her current projects, please visit her website at www.carolericson.com, "where romance flirts with danger."

Visit the Author Profile page at Harlequin.com.

CAST OF CHARACTERS

West Chandler—Dead Falls Island's new sheriff comes with a strong desire to eradicate the drug trade on the island...and a past; when the son of a pretty local Realtor emerges as a possible witness to a murder, West must overcome his past fears and his attraction to the boy's mother to save him.

Astrid Mitchell—As a single mom with a corrupt ex, a former police officer in WITSEC, she has her hands full; when her son becomes entangled in a murder case, she has to turn to another cop for protection, but the new sheriff in town is nothing like her ex.

Olly Crockett—Astrid's son steals the drone his mother borrowed to use for work, but his theft has consequences far worse than a time-out.

Chase Thompson—The murder of this local drug dealer sets off a chain reaction of terrifying events for Astrid and her son.

Naomi Wakefield—Chase's girlfriend may have some ideas about who killed her boyfriend, but will she live long enough to reveal them?

Monique—This mystery woman is connected to Chase in more ways than one, and West needs to find her before she meets the same fate as Naomi and Chase.

Michelle Carter—Astrid's new client shows an avid interest in one of Astrid's listings, a notorious property where a family massacre occurred, and Astrid needs to determine if she's really interested in the property... or its reputation.

Chapter One

Astrid's breath came in short spurts as her gaze darted among the Dead Falls Spring Fling crowd, searching for Olly's bright blond hair. He'd promised to be back before the fair ended. She'd been giving him too much freedom since his father had entered the Federal Witness Protection Program. Just because she couldn't find Russ didn't mean he couldn't find her...and Olly.

"I'm a sucker for sprinkles."

Astrid's head whipped around to confront her customer, a tall, dark and handsome...cop. Her lips stretched into a smile across her gritted teeth. Pointing at the cupcakes arrayed on the trays, she asked, "Vanilla or chocolate frosting?"

He wedged a finger against his impossibly square jaw and cocked his head. "That depends on what's underneath."

"Excuse me?" She raised her eyebrows. Typical cop—always with the flirty double entendre. Did they teach that at the academy? She hadn't seen this deputy around the island. Must be new.

He had the grace to duck his head as a blush touched his cheeks. "I meant the cake part. If the cake is chocolate, I like a vanilla frosting and vice versa."

"You're in luck." She poked a plastic fork in the direction of a chocolate cupcake with white buttercream frosting and sprinkles. "This one is chocolate. I also have carrot cake with a cream cheese frosting."

"Sprinkles?" He ran a hand through his short, dark hair, as if this were the most important decision of his day.

It might very well be, given he belonged to the crack Dead Falls sheriff's department. The residents of the island had been hopeful the new sheriff would turn things around after the disaster of Sheriff Hopkins, but Astrid wasn't holding her breath. Cops—if they weren't inept, they were probably corrupt. At least in her experience.

She sighed. "I can add sprinkles to a carrot cupcake, if you like."

"That would be great…if it's not too much trouble." He took a step back from the table as a middle-aged couple swarmed him.

The woman beamed. "Just wanted to say welcome to Dead Falls Island, Sheriff Chandler. I'm Lydia Feldman, and this is my husband, David."

As Astrid dipped at the knees to grab the plastic bottle of sprinkles, she kept one eye on the exchange between the new sheriff and the Feldmans. So that's why he was at the Spring Fling—meet and mingle with his constituents.

She screwed off the lid of the multicolored sprinkles and shook the bottle over the cream cheese frosting on one of the carrot cupcakes while she watched the new sheriff's easy banter with the couple. He had them wrapped around his little finger.

"Ah, I think that's good." He nodded at the cupcake in the tray, smothered with sprinkles.

"You're the new sheriff." She narrowed her eyes and thrust the cupcake toward him. "That's one dollar."

He carefully took the cupcake from her, the fingers of his left hand pinching the silver sleeve. He extended his right hand. "That's right. West Chandler."

Placing her hand in his, she said, "Astrid Mitchell. Welcome to Dead Falls."

She'd had sprinkles stuck to her fingers and had transferred them to his hand during the shake. They both eyed the sprinkles for an awkward second, their hands still clasped.

"Nice to meet you, Astrid." He slid his hand from hers, sprinkles and all. "Did you make these?"

"Yeah, I did." She wiped her hand on a napkin as if he had cooties. "The Spring Fling is a fundraiser for Samish Elementary, and my son is a student there."

"I knew that—I mean, that this was a fundraiser for the school. It's great to see parents involved in their kids' education. Do you and your husband do a lot of volunteering for the school?" He retrieved a dollar bill from his pocket and handed it to her. Then he peeled back the paper and took a big bite of the cupcake.

She didn't want to talk about her husband, her ex-husband, and a flash of blond hair in the crowd saved her. She waved her hand in the air. "Olly!"

Her son galloped toward her in the booth, his long, skinny legs almost tangling. "Hey, Mom."

"You were gone so long. Where did you end up going?"

He flung his arm out to the side. "You know, just regular places."

He lunged for a cupcake with chocolate frosting, and she smacked his hand. "You have to pay for those. It's a fundraiser."

"I'll get that for him." Sheriff Chandler handed her a crumpled bill.

"Hey, thanks." Olly sank his teeth into the cupcake and asked with his mouth full, "Are you the new sheriff?"

Even her son had figured it out before she had. "This is Sheriff Chandler. Sheriff, this is my son, Olly."

"Good to meet you, Olly." He raised the half-eaten cupcake in the air as he turned away. "Thank you."

Astrid stared after him, the khaki material of his uniform stretched across his broad back as he reached out to shake another hand. He'd only wanted to hit on her and had decided to hightail it out of here as soon as her son showed up. Jerk.

As Olly stuffed the rest of the treat in his mouth, leaving a smear of chocolate on his chin, Astrid noticed his high color and bright eyes. He still hadn't told her what he'd been up to all afternoon while she'd been slaving away at the cupcake booth. "So, where did you and Logan go?"

"Umm, we took our bikes out and rode around, near the cove and stuff." He jabbed a dirty finger at another cupcake. "Can I have that one if I pay you when we get home?"

"Hold on." She turned to Peyton, skipping up to the booth, followed by her mom, Sam. "Hi, you two. Cupcakes?"

"They look delish." Sam patted her curvy hip. "I know I shouldn't, but hey, it's for the school, right?"

"Exactly." Astrid nudged Olly. "Did you say hi to Peyton?"

Olly dropped his chin to his chest, looking up at Peyton through his lashes. "Yeah, hi."

Astrid and Sam exchanged grins as Sam plucked two cupcakes from the tray. Some of the kids were just getting beyond their shyness with the opposite sex, but Peyton and Olly were not among them. Astrid was fine with that. She didn't need to deal with girl problems just yet, not as a single mother.

Peyton swiped her tongue along some vanilla frosting. "I saw you and Logan on your bikes on the cliff over the cove."

"Did not." Olly kicked the leg of the table with the toe of his sneaker, and the remaining cupcakes trembled. Astrid gave him a sharp look from the corner of her eye.

She'd told Olly plenty of times not to ride his bike on the cliff. The lack of guardrails on the edge would result in a sheer drop to the cove.

As Sam peeled back the paper on her cupcake, she asked, "Did you meet the new sheriff? He's here somewhere."

"I did meet him. He bought a cupcake."

"He *is* a cupcake. Or is that beefcake?" Sam wiggled her eyebrows up and down. "And I heard he's single."

"Yeah, he's all right." Astrid stuffed the bills in the cash tin and closed it with a bang. "Let's hope he's better than the last guy."

"Mom." Peyton tugged on Sam's sleeve. "Can we play the game to get a betta fish before they close the booth?"

"Sure. I'll win one for you." Sam gave Astrid a wink before walking away with her daughter.

Still eyeing one of the last of the cupcakes, Olly said, "Fair's almost over, Mom. Can I have that one for free now?"

"You can have it now and pay me later. I baked these to make money for your school, not so you could gobble them all up."

He snatched it up as if he were afraid she'd change her mind.

As she consolidated the remaining cupcakes on one

tray and stacked the other trays, she asked, "Were you and Logan on the cliff above the cove on your bikes today?"

"Peyton doesn't know anything. We weren't up there. Logan's not allowed to ride on the cliff, either." He pulled his cupcake apart at the middle and stuck the bottom half on top of the frosting to make a little cake with icing in the middle. His uncle had taught him that trick.

She decided not to press him but didn't know whether or not to believe him. Ever since she'd told him his father would be away for a long time for his own safety, Olly had been secretive. Her friend Hannah Maddox, who was a child psychologist, told her it was natural for Olly to close down a bit after that news.

Astrid had been trying to give him a little space to process, but she'd been having a hard time of it since her brother, Tate, had left on a special assignment to DC. He'd followed a woman there, and she had no intention of dragging him back here with her whining about Olly. He was her son, and she'd have to raise him as a single mother.

"These are awesome, Mom." Olly rubbed his belly and nodded. "Good job."

She ruffled his shaggy blond hair. "Thanks. Clean your hands off with this sanitizer. Then take this tray with the last of the cupcakes, walk around and try to sell them while I pack up."

She held her breath, expecting pushback, but he squirted a dollop of the clear gel in his palm and vigorously rubbed his hands together. As he grabbed the tray and spun around, she called after him. "And don't try anything sneaky. I know there are seven cupcakes, and I expect seven bucks if you return with an empty tray."

He waved one hand in the air as he delved into the crowd.

Astrid wiped down the table and crouched to grab the box beneath it. She stacked the empty trays inside the box and put the hand sanitizer on top of them, along with a few items she'd brought from home. Lastly, she dropped the plastic bottle of sprinkles in the box.

The new sheriff sure did like his sprinkles but didn't seem to like kids much, or he didn't like women with kids. Sam had mentioned he was single, so that explained a lot. Not that Astrid was looking to date anyone, but if she did, she always thought going out with a divorced dad with kids might be easier than trying to hit a bachelor over the head with family life right out of the box.

She slipped her phone from the pocket of her denim jacket. It might be spring in Dead Falls, but the winter chill hadn't quite dissipated. She tapped Kelsey Monroe in her contacts. Kelsey was the PTA treasurer and all-around volunteer queen.

"Hi, Kelsey. It's Astrid Mitchell. I'm about ready to close down the cupcake booth. Do you want to pick up the money now, or should I drop it off later?"

Out of breath, as usual, Kelsey said, "I'm just picking up the money from the hot dog booth. I'll be right over."

By the time Astrid finished counting the money, Kelsey scurried up, a large duffel bag over her shoulder, weighing her petite frame down on one side. Kelsey flashed a set of dimples. "Your cupcakes were a smashing success. Everyone was raving about them—even the new sheriff."

Astrid cleared her throat. "Good to hear. I sent Olly out to sell the remaining ones. If he comes back with any more money, I can drop it off in your mailbox."

"Perfect." Kelsey shook out a zippered money pouch and

produced a sticky note and a felt pen. "Just write down the amount here and stuff the money in the bag."

As Astrid began to scribble the total for the cupcakes, Olly ran up to them, panting and waving a ten-dollar bill in the air. "Mom, Mom. Sheriff Chandler bought all the cupcakes left on the tray, gave me ten bucks for them and handed them out to some kids leaving the fair."

"Isn't that nice?" Kelsey's cheeks turned pink. "I like him better than Sheriff Hopkins already."

Astrid crossed out the previous amount she'd written and added ten to it. So, Chandler did like kids—just not hers. "He overpaid. There were only seven left."

"Well, I like him even more then." Kelsey zipped up the money bag and dropped it in the duffel with the others. "I think this was a great success, and even the weather held."

Astrid and Olly finished clearing the booth, and she made him carry the box of supplies to the car. Tate had left his Jeep behind when he went to DC, but she preferred her truck although she knew she'd have to trade up if she wanted to be a successful Realtor on the island. Nobody wanted to see a Realtor pull up in a beat-up old pickup.

Olly loaded the box in the truck bed and joined her in the cab. The sugar from the two cupcakes—maybe three— had made him hyper and he yakked in the seat beside her about the games he'd played and the friends he'd seen at the Spring Fling. She let him chatter on during the ride, enjoying his vivacity after a few months of morose silence.

She pulled the truck in front of Tate's cabin, as he'd in-sisted on calling it, despite its size, comfort and amenities. Olly had the door open before she even killed the engine.

As she stepped out of the truck, she called him back. "Hey, get the box out of the back."

He scampered past her and dived into the back head-first. He then followed her up the porch to the front door, hopping from one foot to the other. He either had to pee or she was facing a long night ahead getting him down from his sugar rush.

She slid the key into the door lock, and then shoved it into the deadbolt lock. It didn't click over, and she tsked her tongue. Had she forgotten to lock the dead bolt?

Bumping the door with her hip, she reached for the security keypad. Her fingers rested against the display with the red light. Had she forgotten to set the security, too? She must've been in a rush this morning.

She tapped the side of the box in Olly's arms. "Take this to the kitchen, and we'll put away the stuff."

She followed him to the kitchen, where he dropped the box on the floor, the metal trays clanging.

"Hey, be careful with that."

"L-look, Mom."

She raised her head to follow his pointing finger and gasped at the broken glass from the side door. She grabbed Olly, digging her fingers into his bony shoulder. "We need to get out now."

Chapter Two

West took a sip of coffee as he stared at the falls, the flavor bitter on his tongue after those sweet cupcakes. His intermittent wipers kept up with the mist that collected on his windshield—barely. He could do this. New job. New town. New start.

After the previous sheriff of Dead Falls Island, the city council had welcomed his urban experience. The small town had recently suffered through a couple of murders and kidnappings, and its location near the Canadian border had put it on the map for the drug trade.

That's how the council members had tried to sell him on the job, by pumping up the excitement and danger. Although a few dead bodies and missing kids couldn't compare to the volume of crime he dealt with in Chicago, he'd taken the job to escape that level of violence and mayhem—to escape the violence in himself before it overwhelmed him.

The Spring Fling had been the perfect opportunity for him to meet and greet the community and enjoy some awesome food. He licked his lips, still tasting the buttery frosting from that cupcake. He didn't know what Astrid did for a living but if she made those cupcakes, she had a future as a baker. She fit right in with the island—tall, athletically slim, fresh-faced with eyes that matched the color of Discovery Bay. When he'd looked into those eyes, he'd felt something he hadn't felt in almost two years. Too bad she had a kid, especially that kid.

The radio in his unmarked SUV crackled to life, and the dispatcher's voice called out a break-in. In Chicago, that call wouldn't even warrant radio chatter. He checked the address on his GPS and discovered he was close to the location. Might as well jump in with both feet. The town had complained about the previous sheriff's laziness, his unwillingness to get involved in the crimes on the island. West had never suffered from indolence, so he got on the radio and indicated he'd respond to the call.

He stashed his coffee cup in the holder and peeled away from the Dead Falls overlook. He didn't exactly have to go code four. Apparently, the burglars hadn't made an appearance yet, but he owed it to the frightened homeowner to get there as soon as he could. The beauty of small-town service and all that.

He followed his GPS back across the bridge and farther into the woods, taking a small road that led to a large cabin—house.

A woman stood at the edge of the drive, clutching a shovel in both hands, her blond hair over one shoulder, a boy standing to the side, kicking a log. West swallowed hard. Had he conjured up Astrid and her son from his thoughts?

He parked his car several feet behind them, down the drive from the glass-and-wood cabin with its wraparound porch and alpine roof. The views from the house must be spectacular.

He stepped out of the car, his boot crunching gravel and dirt. Lifting his hand, he said, "Are you both okay?"

"We're fine." Astrid clamped a hand on Olly's shoulder. "Stop kicking that."

"Any sign of the intruders?" He approached them, his hands relaxed at his sides, away from his holster.

"We didn't see anyone. As soon as I noticed the broken window in the kitchen, we left." She pounded the shovel into the ground. "We made it this far, and I haven't seen anyone leave the house. Of course, they could've slipped out the back and disappeared into the forest."

West's gaze tracked around the perimeter of the house, taking in the greenery on all sides. A barbecue and firepit nestled on one side of the house in a clearing.

He flung his arm at the house. "I can go inside on my own first, if you like, to make sure it's all clear. Then you can join me and let me know if anything is missing. I can have a forensics person out here to dust for prints near the broken window."

She bit her bottom lip and then shrugged. "Sure. That's fine. We'll follow you. I left the front door open when we ran outside."

West strode to the front of the house, his hand hovering over his weapon, Astrid and Olly a safe distance behind. He nudged the door open with his shoulder. He didn't want to add his own prints to the mix.

A quick check of the house confirmed the burglars had vacated the premises. He stepped onto the porch and waved at Astrid and Olly, stationed next to a white truck. "Nobody here."

Astrid hoisted the shovel into the truck bed and marched to the porch. "I can't believe someone got in here. I must've forgotten to set the alarm when I left for the Spring Fling— too preoccupied."

"Cameras?" West jabbed a finger at a camera tucked under the eaves.

"Yes, but not by the side door, which is where they entered. If the security system had been set, the alarm would've sounded when the intruders broke into that window on the side door."

West shook his head. "I'm sorry. Security systems are only useful when they're properly set."

Astrid wedged a hand on her hip. "No kidding. I'll check to see if anything's missing. My brother keeps guns and other items in his safe. I'd better have a look there first."

"Your brother?" His eyes flickered to a black Jeep parked in front of the truck. "You live with your brother?"

"Temporarily, and he's off the island for several months." She held up one finger. "Wait here, and I'll run upstairs to check the safe."

Olly perched on the arm of the sofa when his mom left the room. The boy studied the gun in his holster, and a bead of sweat trickled down West's back.

"My dad's a cop."

West licked his lips. "Really? Do you know what department he works for?"

"I dunno." Olly hunched his skinny shoulders. "He's hiding right now."

West widened his eyes but before he could respond, Astrid jogged down the stairs.

"Safe is untouched, same for my jewelry box." She crooked a finger. "Did you see how they got in?"

He followed her into the kitchen, where she stopped short of the broken glass on the hardwood floor. Whoever broke in had closed the door behind them, but they had busted out the top window and reached in to unlock and open the door.

Pivoting from the mess on the floor, he asked, "Do you want to have a look around down here? Any cash lying around? Expensive gadgets? Looks like maybe a quick smash-and-grab."

"Uh-oh." Astrid covered her mouth with one hand and pushed past him into the step-down living room with the massive stone fireplace and a wall of windows that framed the forest and the bay beyond. She stopped at the coffee table and picked up the single book resting on the shiny wood.

Her head cranked from side to side, and she lunged at the large sectional sofa, grabbing pillows and tossing them aside. "I can't believe this."

"There *is* something missing?" And by Astrid's frantic movements and flushed cheeks, he'd have to guess the intruders took something important or expensive…or both.

"The drone. My company's drone is missing." She threw her hands up in the air. "Olly, did you see it before we left? Didn't I put it on the coffee table?"

Astrid's emotions had gotten to her son. His face paled so that his freckles stood out on his nose as he twisted his fingers in front of him. "I-I think so, Mom. It was right there on the table."

"Your company?" West took a turn around the room, scanning the well-ordered surfaces for the high-tech gadget.

"I'm a Realtor. I just recently got my license and started working for Discovery Bay Realty on the island. I'm putting together a package for a listing and borrowed the drone to get some aerial shots. This is bad." She continued upending cushions and peering under the furniture that couldn't possibly hide a drone.

"I'm sorry. Your company probably has insurance. Maybe it won't be a huge loss for them. You can file a police report, and Discovery Bay Realty can send that along to the insurance company." He wanted to put his hands on her shoulders to steady her, to calm her agitated movements.

"A police report?" Olly's eyes rounded into saucers, taking up most of his thin face. "Is that against the law?"

"Of course it is, Olly." Astrid threw her arms out to her sides. "It's burglary. It's theft."

West cleared his throat. "Is there anything else missing? If they grabbed the drone, they may have made off with similar easy to carry items. Cameras? Phones? Watches? Artwork?"

Astrid crossed the room to some shelving and ran her finger along the edge of each shelf, filled with objets d'art. "Some of these pieces are kind of expensive, but I don't notice anything gone. A lot of my possessions are in storage, and I'm not sure about Tate's stuff. I don't think he has a camera."

"Keep looking. If you spot anything else out of the ordinary, we can add it to the police report. I'll try to get a fingerprint tech out here from forensics to check that door and window, maybe the coffee table if you really think that's where you left the drone." Out of the corner of his eye, West saw Olly scampering toward the kitchen. "Whoa, there, buddy. Where are you going? You'll want to stay away from that door and broken window for now."

Olly tripped to a stop and spun around, his movements jerky. Poor kid was taking this hard.

"What about my bike, Mom? Maybe they took my bike. I was gonna go out to the side of the house where I left it."

Astrid pointed to the wall of windows and a door tucked into the corner. "Go out the back way for now."

When Olly rushed outside, Astrid rubbed her arms. "He seems upset. Maybe I should've sent him out of the house. He's had some…upsets lately."

Like his missing father?

West pulled his phone from his pocket. "I'll give the station a call to find out when the tech can get here. You can drop by any time to fill out the report. The sooner the better. Hey, if anyone starts playing with a drone around here, maybe we can recover it. It might even have a GPS tracker on it, if we're lucky."

"I was thinking about that." She turned toward him, extending her hand. "Thanks so much…"

Like a magnet, he went to her, a loud yell from outside stopping his progress.

"Mom! Mom, I found it!"

Astrid's eyes popped open as she glanced at West. "Thank goodness."

She made her way to the back door, and West followed her. This had to be the strangest burglary ever. They almost collided with Olly rounding the corner of the house at warp speed, his arms wrapped around a large box.

He pulled up short in front of them, panting and patting the box. "Look. I found it."

"Let me take that. It's heavy." Astrid scooped the box from Olly's arms. "Where in the world did you find it?"

"Umm—" Olly jerked a thumb over his shoulder "—it was in the garbage can. I left my bike next to the cans, so when I went to look for my bike, I saw the lid off the can and the box stuck in there."

West cocked his head. "That's strange. Could've been

kids who got spooked and dumped it in the trash before they took off."

"Probably, unless something else was taken." Astrid asked Olly, "Did you see anything else in the trash can or on the side of the house with your bike?"

"No." Olly put his arms behind him and rocked back on his heels.

Astrid screwed up one side of her mouth. "Did you notice anything out there when you rode your bike home? Before Mrs. Davidson gave you a ride to the Spring Fling?"

"No." Olly pressed his lips together, for some reason determined to give his mother as little information as possible.

"Let me take this inside." She hoisted the box in her arms. "It's getting heavy."

"I'll take it." West placed his hands beneath the box, as his eyes met Astrid's over the top. She released it quickly before he had a handle on it, and he stepped back to gain a little purchase so he wouldn't end up dropping the drone and getting her in trouble with her employer all over again.

He stamped his feet before walking back into the house and its gleaming hardwood floors. "On the table?"

"Yes, please."

Olly trailed behind them. As her son closed the door, Astrid came up behind him and wrapped her arms around him. "Thank you. Olly. If you'd never gone to look at your bike, I probably wouldn't have found the drone until trash day."

The boy's face brightened. "Does that mean I can play Xbox before dinner?"

"Go ahead." She tousled his blond mane. "But you're done when I say you're done. You're not going to waste your spring break in front of the tube."

"Okay, Mom." He turned at the bottom of the staircase and raised a hand. "Bye, Sheriff Chandler."

"See ya, Olly. Good detective work."

Olly grinned and hopped up the stairs, two at a time.

West stared after him, scratching his chin. "That was... lucky."

"Maybe not. I'd better call my brother and send him some pictures to see if anything else is missing, but if the thieves crammed the drone in the trash can, I'm thinking it was some teens who got cold feet."

"Whether or not anything is missing, you still need to report it. You can probably make a claim on your home-owners' insurance to get reimbursed for the door."

"Good idea." She waved a finger at him. "See, you're better than Sheriff Hopkins already."

"From what I understand, not such big shoes to fill, but I'll take the compliment." The phone in his pocket rang, and he checked the display. "Excuse me. It's the station. I need to take this."

"I'll sweep up this glass, if that's okay."

He nodded as he fished the phone from his pocket. "Chandler."

"Sheriff, this is George Vickers. We just got a call, and I think you're gonna want to be there for this."

West glanced at Astrid sweeping up the glass on the kitchen floor and rolled his eyes. Was this one going to be a kitten up a tree?

"Yeah, what is it, Vickers?"

"Dog walkers just discovered a dead body at the cove—Crystal Cove."

"On my way." West tapped the phone against his chin before sliding it into his pocket. "So, not a cat up a tree."

Chapter Three

Wiping her hands on a dish towel, Astrid strolled back into the living room, catching the sheriff talking to himself. "Everything okay? If you have to leave, I think we're done here. I'll check with my brother to find out if any items are missing, and I'll go to the station tomorrow to file the police report."

He pocketed his phone and made a move for the door, all of a sudden in a big hurry to take off—kind of like this afternoon. "Yeah, I do have to get going. Not sure I'll be able to get the fingerprint tech out here to dust the side door or the drone box."

"Oh, well—" she bunched the towel in her hands "—that's okay. Olly and I can avoid using that door, but I'll have to get the window replaced tonight."

"Do what you have to do to be safe." He bolted for the front door, not even waiting for her to show him out. He called over his shoulder. "Glad Olly found the drone."

"Yeah, me, too." She strode after him and grabbed the door when he flung it open. "Thanks for all your help, Sheriff Chandler."

"West." Without turning around, he waved a hand in the air on his way to his black SUV.

She closed the door behind him, locked it and set the security system, that broken window in the kitchen relegating the act to a useless gesture. Sheriff Chandler... West had practically run from the house. Just another unstable cop, even though his sincere good guy act had her going there for a while.

Sighing, she used the dish towel to open the back door and carried the dustpan full of glass to the trash cans on the side of the house. She maneuvered around Olly's bike leaning up against the wall and tipped the lid off the first can. She dumped the glass on top of a few plastic garbage bags in the bottom of the can.

She tilted her head. Had Olly found the drone in this one? There wasn't enough trash in here to make the drone box sit on top with a skewed lid. Isn't that what he'd said? No, maybe he'd said the whole lid was off.

She peeked into the can, which was half full. The intruders must've had a change of heart.

As she walked back into the house, her phone on the counter started buzzing. She checked the display as she picked it up. "Hey, Sam. Did you forget something at the Spring Fling?"

"Oh my God, Astrid, did you hear about the dead body?"

Astrid sucked in a short breath. "Dead body? On the island? Oh God, it's not another one of Dr. Summers' victims from his killing spree years ago, is it? I thought we'd found and accounted for all those missing kids. I'll have to tell Tate."

Sam lowered her voice to a whisper. "No, this is a current murder, an adult male. Someone walking a dog at the cove discovered him just this afternoon."

"Why are you whispering?" Astrid pressed her fingers against her chin. "Wait, at the cove? Crystal Cove?"

"Yeah, down by the water." Sam cleared her throat. "I was whispering because Peyton decided to come into the kitchen for a snack."

Astrid flickered her gaze to the ceiling, hoping Olly was too immersed in his game to come downstairs. "What time was the body found? Olly and Logan were out at the cove today before Logan's mom dropped him off at the Fling."

"Not sure." Sam lowered her voice again. "I think it's a drug thing. You know how shady the cove is."

"How do you know all this already? How do you know it's not just a drowning instead of a murder?"

"Well, I *do* live near the cove. Kinda hard to miss the sirens and emergency vehicles flying up the road, and the rumor's out there that the victim was shot—so no drowning." Sam smacked her lips. "I even saw the hot new sheriff."

"Stop calling him that." Astrid's cheeks flamed, and she was glad Sam was on audio only and not video chat. "He was actually at my house when he got the call, but he kept mum about it."

Chandler had hightailed it out of here on his way to the murder scene without telling her a thing. He obviously didn't understand how small towns worked if he thought she wouldn't find out within hours—actually minutes—of the discovery of a dead body.

"Wait, what? The hot sheriff was at your house already? Girl, I thought you'd had it with cops."

"Stop." Astrid perched on the edge of a stool at the kitchen island. "Someone broke into my house today."

"Really?" Sam clicked her tongue. "I swear, this island is suffering an absolute crime wave. What the hell? Did the little punks steal anything?"

"You're already blaming the teens."

"Yeah, those Goth, Wiccan punks who skulk around in their black clothes."

Astrid snorted out a laugh. "I doubt they spend their time breaking into homes. Too busy with incantations in the forest. Anyway, I didn't notice anything gone, but I'll have to check with Tate."

"I'm going to head out there with the rest of the lookie-loos. You wanna join me? We could have a cocktail or two in town after. We worked hard on that damned Spring Fling, and the kids are out on break. We deserve it."

Astrid rolled her shoulders, feeling the tension of the day. "I'd take you up on it, but I'm not dragging Olly out to a crime scene."

"I've got that covered. My mom is coming in a few to boil eggs with Peyton for the Easter egg hunt. She's ordering pizza and everything. Olly can join them." Sam had added a singsong, cajoling tone to her last sentence.

"Okay, we're in. I have to warn you that Olly still thinks Peyton is kind of icky, but he'll be down for boiling eggs and pizza for sure."

"Great. Pro tip. Break off the main road and come up the back way to our house, so Olly doesn't see all the hoopla. I told Peyton some lie about the sirens."

"Gotcha. You're such a good mom." Astrid glanced at the side door. "I do need some time to board up my window. It's broken."

"I'll send Anton over to do that. He needs the work anyway, and he's out your way right now. I'll text him, and he can work on it while you're over here."

"If you're sure."

"Bruce is trying to worm his way back into my life, so his son knows he has to jump when I whistle."

"Must be nice. Tell your stepson I'll give him a bonus for coming out after hours and if this will help you and Bruce fix your marriage, I'm all for it."

"Whose side are you on?"

"Yours. I'll be there in about thirty minutes."

Thirty-five minutes later, she took the back road to Sam's house in a newish tract of homes near the coast, walking distance to Crystal Cove. Olly had whined about leaving his game and whined some more about going to a *girl's* house, but the promise of pizza mollified him.

She'd avoided the emergency vehicles Sam had warned her about on the phone. Would they still be there? West had left her house about an hour ago. If this were a murder, even an accident, the cops would be on the scene for a long time.

She pulled into Sam's driveway, behind her car, and put her hand on Olly's shoulder as he reached for the door. "Remember, be nice to Peyton. This is her house, and we're guests."

"All right, but she'd better not tell anyone I was over here doing Easter eggs with her." Olly jutted his chin out and tumbled from the car.

Rolling her eyes, Astrid followed. She had to remember that this stage was probably preferable to make-out sessions behind Dead Falls. By the time she reached the door, Olly had already rung the bell, and Sam swung it open.

"Hello, you two. You're just in time. Luigi's delivered the pizzas a few minutes ago, and the hard-boiled eggs are cooling and ready to color."

Astrid raised a hand at Sam's mother, Lucy, and Peyton sitting in the living room playing a game of go fish. "Hi, Lucy. How are you?"

"Losing." She slapped a card onto the coffee table in front of Peyton. "Olly, do you want to join us?"

Olly glanced at the three pizza boxes on the counter, caught his mom's eye and said, "Okay."

Sam said, "Don't worry, Olly. We'll bring the pizza to you."

"I'll get the plates." Astrid turned toward the cupboard, but Sam whipped a stack of paper plates from a plastic bag.

"No dishes tonight. I'm on spring break."

Peyton shoved her glasses up the bridge of her nose with her thumb. "You promised soda tonight, Mom."

"I did." Sam mouthed the word *sorry* to Astrid and said aloud, "Is that okay with you, Astrid?"

"Please, Mom." Olly bounced up and down on the couch. A soda was going to send this kid into overdrive.

"I suppose. You've already had about twenty cupcakes, what's a cup or so more of sugar." Astrid stuck out her tongue at Sam.

The kids clapped like a couple of trained seals, and Astrid murmured to Sam. "Are you sure your mom's up for this?"

She winked. "Dad was a prison guard. I'm sure she learned a few tricks from him."

"I heard that, Sam." Lucy snapped her fingers. "And when you bring those sodas out here, bring me a glass of red while you're at it."

"That's how she gets through." Sam nudged Astrid with her elbow.

Astrid took the pizza orders—cheese for Peyton, pepperoni for Olly and the deluxe for Lucy. She surveyed the three open boxes. "You have enough pizza here to feed an army."

Tapping her head, her springy curls bouncing, Sam said, "Ready-made breakfast. I'm always thinking."

When they delivered the food and drinks to Lucy and the kids in the living room, Sam and Astrid settled at the kitchen table with their own slices and sodas.

Lucy raised her glass. "You two not imbibing?"

"We're going to have a drink in town." Sam cracked open her soda. "If that's okay with you, Mom."

"That's fine. Just avoid the cove." Lucy took a sip of her wine, and Sam sliced a finger across her throat.

Olly choked on his soda and wiped the back of his hand beneath his nose. "What's wrong with the cove?"

"I think there was some debris on the beach from a slide." Astrid raised her eyebrows at Sam, who nodded. They'd better get their stories straight. Kids always had a sense when you were lying.

"Olly was at the cove today. On the cliff." Peyton nipped off the point of her cheese pizza with her teeth and then daintily dabbed a napkin to her lips.

"We rode by. We weren't on the cliff." Olly scowled at Peyton and shoved some pizza into his mouth, chewing loudly in her direction.

Astrid snapped at him. "Olly. Manners, please. I'm just going to tell you again. You're not allowed on that cliff above the cove."

"I know. Me and Logan just rode past."

By the time the kids finished their pizza, they'd made a truce and when Lucy told them the eggs had cooled off enough to color, they were practically best friends.

Sam must've figured this was the perfect time to make their escape, as she jerked her thumb at the door. They left Lucy and the kids huddled around the kitchen table dropping colored tabs into bowls under fumes of vinegar.

When they walked outside, they skirted Astrid's truck in the driveway and crossed the street to make their way to Crystal Cove. Astrid pulled her jacket closed as she followed Sam on a narrow trail through a small patch of woods that led down to the rocky beach. People didn't sunbathe at Crystal Cove, even when it got warm enough to do so. They explored the tide pools, took their chances in the caves at low tide and launched boats from the deep-water inlet—usually for nefarious purposes.

A few dead bodies had wound up on the beach from misadventures on the cliff above. That's why she'd given Olly strict instructions to say away from the cliff. He could ride his bike right over the edge and sail onto the beach.

As they clumped down the end of the trail, voices carried back to them, muffled by the trees. Watching the ground for gnarled roots, Astrid almost bumped into Sam when she stopped short.

"I guess we're not getting any closer." Sam waved her hand toward a line of yellow tape stretched between two trees, keeping people off the beach.

Astrid peered around her at the clutch of people where the trail met the sand, craning their necks. She nudged Sam in the back. "Let's find out what they know. I see Charlene Lundstrom. She probably got here to stick her nose in before half of the sheriff's department arrived."

Sam twisted her head over her shoulder. "If Charlene is sticking her nose in, what are *we* doing?"

"Taking a leisurely stroll." She gave Sam a little push between the shoulder blades. "Move it."

They joined the other lookie-loos, the toes of their shoes

touching the sand of the beach. Astrid shoved her hands in the pockets of her jacket and nodded at Charlene. "Do we know who he is?"

Charlene clutched at her sweater. "It's a local."

"A local?" Astrid's pulse ticked up a few notches. "Who is it?"

Charlene's husband spoke without turning around. "It's that Chase Thompson, so probably drug-related."

Astrid bit her lip. Chase was a local, small-time drug dealer. He must've upped his game to warrant a murder at Crystal Cove.

Standing on her tiptoes, Sam said, "I heard he was shot. Is that right?"

A few other people gathered around murmured their assent.

Peering upward at the cliff's edge, Astrid said to no one in particular, "So, he didn't fall from the cliff."

Kevin Badgley, a local fisherman, crossed his arms and leaned against the trunk of a tree. "My guess is Chase was either expecting to shove off in a boat, or he just landed with some drugs and was intercepted. Either way, the new sheriff had better make some inroads into drug trafficking in Discovery Bay. The back-and-forth with the Canadian border is only getting worse."

"Is he here—Sheriff Chandler?" Astrid stood on her tiptoes and scanned the emergency personnel gathered on the beach.

"I think he's still with the body, which we can't see from here." Charlene almost sounded disappointed.

"There he is." Sam jabbed Astrid with a sharp elbow, and Astrid rubbed her arm.

West had walked up from the water and was talking

and gesturing to one of the uniforms on the sand. As he glanced at the crowd of people at the edge of the beach, Astrid ducked behind the solid form of Kevin.

She hissed at Sam. "Let's go."

"Oh, you don't want him to see you snooping around a crime scene?" Sam fanned her face. "Whatever will he think of you."

"I'm leaving." Astrid spun around and clumped back up the trail. She huffed out a breath. "You'd better follow me if you want a ride to the bar."

Sam scrambled after her and hooked a finger in her belt loop. "Lead the way."

When they reached Sam's house, Sam peeked into the window to make sure her mother and the kids were still coloring eggs. Then Astrid drove into town and parked on the main street halfway between the only two bars still open.

"Let's see." Sam wedged a finger against her chin. "Dive bar extraordinaire the Salty Crab, or *upscale* prosecco at the bar at the Grill?"

Astrid snorted. "I refuse to go into the Salty Crab with you. Last time we were there, you almost got into a fight."

"I had an excuse. I'd just found out Bruce was sexting with that…woman."

"That was not sexting, but I'm still not showing my face in there." Astrid shoved open the door of the truck. "The Grill, it is."

Sam joined her on the sidewalk. "We'd probably get more info about Chase in the Salty Crab."

"Don't care." Astrid hooked her arm through Sam's. "This way, missy."

The Grill was about to close the kitchen for dinner, but

the bar would remain open for another few hours. Astrid steered her friend into a cozy booth by the window.

When their waitress got to their table, she said, "The kitchen is about to close, but I can get you some food."

Sam waved her hand in the air. "We just had a bunch of pizza, but you can bring me a glass of the house red."

"Same." Astrid raised her hand.

After they settled in with their drinks and speculated about Chase Thompson's death, Astrid nursed her wine while watching Sam down three of the same as she complained about her husband.

Astrid didn't dare tell Sam some of the stuff her husband Russ pulled. Unlike Astrid's own husband, Sam's was a good guy despite his misstep.

Sam took a breath and tapped her phone. "Should I call Mom and find out how the kids are doing?"

"Sure, let her know we'll be back soon. I'm ready to wrap it up." Astrid put a finger in the air to catch the waitress's attention.

Scooting out of the booth and tossing a card on the table, Sam said, "I'm going to hit the ladies' room. My treat 'cuz I outdrank you three to one."

Sam disappeared down the dark hallway to the restrooms, and Astrid held up her friend's credit card for the waitress.

When Sam returned, she tipped the dregs of her third glass of wine down her throat. "Mom said the kids crashed out on the couch watching TV. She took Peyton up to bed and tucked a blanket around Olly. He can sleep over, if you like. Then you don't have to disturb him and try to get him to sleep again when you get home."

"That's okay. I'm driving you home, anyway. Might as well scoop him up while I'm there."

Sam fluffed up her curls. "You're tall, but Olly is almost up to your shoulder already. I doubt you can scoop up that boy anymore."

When the waitress returned with the card, Sam's eyes widened as she gazed past her shoulder. "What are you doing here, Anton? You're not twenty-one yet."

"Mama Lucy told me where you were and I was eating a burger at Gus's anyway, so I just wanted to let Ms. Mitchell know that I boarded up the glass in her door."

"Thanks, Anton. I'll pay you online when I get home."

"No hurry." He pulled his hat over his short Afro. "Did you hear about Chase Thompson down at the cove?"

"We did." Sam gave an exaggerated shiver. "That's why your dad and I are always nagging you to stay away from drugs. Bad news."

"My friends and I aren't into drugs, Sam. I told you guys that."

"We still worry." Sam snapped her fingers. "Hey, are you going home now? Can you give me a ride? That way Astrid doesn't have to, and Olly can sleep over."

Anton answered, "Yeah, I'm on my way home."

"Only if you're sure it's okay, Sam. I don't want Olly to spoil your plans tomorrow."

"I don't have any plans tomorrow." Sam grabbed her jacket. "It's settled. You can pick him up in the morning."

"Okay, thanks." Astrid patted Anton's arm. "And thank you for fixing my window."

"No problem, Ms. Mitchell."

Astrid grabbed her own jacket. "You two go ahead. I'm going to use the restroom."

They said their goodbyes, and Astrid made her way to the back of the bar, which had cleared during their chat session. When she finished in the ladies' room, she walked through the bar toward the front door, waving to the bartender and the waitress.

Once outside, she plunged her hand into her purse for her keys and strode toward her truck, which sat alone at the curb. This end of downtown Dead Falls rolled up the sidewalks early, even on weekends. The Salty Crab on the other end of the street kept its doors open until two, and several cars were still bunched up in front of the squat building with a pink neon crab on the front. Classy place.

As she approached her truck, the low heels of her boots clicking on the pavement, a dark figure emerged from the truck bed.

She squinted and called out. "That's my truck. What are you doing?"

Gripping her keys between her fingers, her adrenaline pumping her legs, she ran toward the truck. Before she could reach the bumper, the person jumped from the truck bed, swinging something in his hand.

She managed a strangled cry before a sharp pain pierced her brain and everything went dark.

Chapter Four

West rubbed his eyes and sucked down the rest of his Coke. First week on the job and a dead body on the beach. He slapped a five on the bar for the drink and nodded his thanks at the bartender. He hadn't wanted Chicago-level crime, but he didn't want to fall asleep on the job, either.

The Salty Crab, Chase Thompson's favorite hangout, hadn't yielded much in the way of information. Chase's friends had kept mum about the dead man's activities prior to his death, but West planned to dig so deep into their own personal affairs, those friends would come around eventually.

He twisted around on his barstool, eyeing his company, some loudly arguing in the corner, a few playing pool and one guy trying his luck with a couple of women at the jukebox. If this motley crew stayed until closing time, he hoped they had alternate transportation home.

Brayden Phelps, one of the guys West had questioned earlier, stumbled back into the bar through the front door. "Hey, there's a dead chick on the sidewalk."

West shoved back from the bar, his heart hammering. No way did Dead Falls produce two dead bodies his first week of work.

He strode toward Brayden, who was pitching and weaving. The guy was so drunk, he probably didn't know what he saw.

Grabbing Brayden's sleeve, West said, "Show me."

Brayden staggered outside. Obviously, the shock of seeing a dead body hadn't sobered him up. Half the bar cleared out behind them as Brayden pointed down the street at a lone truck parked in the shadows.

Brayden's finger wavered. "Right there. She's behind the truck."

West's mouth went dry. He'd seen that truck before—at Astrid's cabin. He shoved Brayden out of the way and jogged down the sidewalk toward the truck.

He saw a pair of feet in some low-heeled boots propped up on the curb before he saw the rest of the body in the street behind the truck. Astrid's blond hair fanned out behind her on the asphalt.

He crouched beside her, his fingers reaching for the pulse in her throat. When he saw her chest rise and fall, her eyelashes flutter, he finally breathed.

As the bar patrons crowded behind him, he said over his shoulder, "Stay back. Don't touch anything."

"She ain't dead." Brayden hiccupped at his audience. "Prolly hammered."

The pulse beneath his fingertips beat strong and sure, and he scanned her body for an injury. "Astrid? Can you hear me? It's Sheriff Chandler."

A moan escaped from her parted lips, and she raised a hand to her head.

"Are you injured? Can you sit up?" West fumbled for the phone in his pocket and called 911. If she needed medical treatment, he wanted the EMTs here as soon as possible.

She mumbled something and slid her fingers along the

back of her scalp. His flashlight picked up dark wet streaks on her palm.

He shouted. "Someone run back to the bar and get a clean cloth from the bartender—a couple."

Astrid struggled to sit up, and West curled an arm under her back to support her. She leaned into him, and even the blood and the oil and grime from the road couldn't diminish the fresh citrus scent from her bright locks. He also smelled the deeper fruity scent of wine on her breath.

"An ambulance is on the way. Did you fall and hit your head?" He turned to the side and flicked his flashlight at the bumper of the truck. Had she hit her head on the truck on her way down?

She sucked a breath in through her teeth. "Didn't fall. Someone attacked me. Hit me on the back of the head with something…hard."

As the bartender from the Salty Crab shoved two white towels at him, he said, "Hey, Sheriff. There's glass all over the road on the driver side of the truck. Looks like a broken window."

"Yeah, don't touch it." West bunched up one of the towels and pressed it gently against the back of her head. "Here?"

Astrid hissed. "Toward my right."

As sirens whooped down the street, West clenched his jaw. Someone breaks into Astrid's house and now her truck? He didn't believe in coincidences like this. Was there something Astrid had neglected to tell him earlier? Did she have enemies? Did her husband have enemies?

"Did you get a look at the person or persons who attacked you?"

She shifted her head. "One guy. He had a mask over his

face. At first, I just thought it was too dark to see, but he definitely had a mask on."

An ambulance pulled up behind the truck, followed by a patrol unit. This time, he planned to do a little more investigating. He waved his hand in the air at the EMTs as they jumped from their emergency vehicle.

The taller EMT got a hitch in his step when he approached the scene. "Sheriff Chandler."

"Have a look at Astrid. Someone hit her over the head. Knocked her out."

"I never lost consciousness." Astrid dug a hand into his shoulder to haul herself to her feet and promptly swayed.

West popped up beside her and put a light hand on her hip. Tapping the back of his head, he said, "There's a wound here."

"Can you walk, Astrid?" The second EMT took her arm. "Come to the back of the ambulance. We'll treat you there."

"Of course I can walk." She took a few careful steps toward the ambulance.

When West saw her seated on the back, the two EMTs attending to her, he approached one of the patrol officers. "Deputy Robard, you're trained in printing, correct?"

Robard flicked her ponytail over her shoulder. "Yes, sir. We have a kit in the back."

"Just for the heck of it, can you dust the truck? The guy broke in through the driver's-side window before attacking Astrid. She's not sure what he used to hit her, but it might be in the bed. That's where he was when she approached her truck."

She jerked her chin toward Astrid. "Is she okay? It's just that she's been through a lot lately, and her brother's out of town right now."

West cocked his head. "You know about the break-in at her place?"

"What? No." Robard widened her dark eyes. "I should probably call her brother, who's a friend of mine, but she'd kill me if I did."

"Let's just see if we can figure out who's targeting her." He jerked his thumb at the truck, and the female deputy strode back to the patrol car.

Less than an hour later, Astrid's truck had been dusted for prints and her wound dressed. The crowd from the Salty Crab had dispersed, and the EMTs were wrapping up.

Astrid stood next to her truck, kicking at the glass in the street with the toe of her boot.

"We got prints this time, just in case."

"I noticed." She wrinkled her nose, eyeing the smudges on her truck.

"That'll come off easily." He cleared his throat. "Are you okay to drive home? Where's your son?"

"He's at an impromptu sleepover, and I'm fine."

"You did lose consciousness, you know. That guy who came running into the bar thought you were dead."

"He was probably drunk if he was out at this hour." She rolled her eyes and winced. Touching the edge of her bandage, she said, "You're right. I did black out, but just for a few minutes. I guess my attacker just wanted what was in my truck."

"But you said he didn't take anything from your truck. Do you need to have another look? Or maybe save it for tomorrow when you're feeling better?"

Her gaze darted to the bed of her truck. "He did break into the tool caddy. He might've taken something out of there. I'll go through it tomorrow."

"Someone breaks into your house, takes the drone, thinks better of it and leaves it in the trash can. Then that same person, or someone else, breaks into your truck and doesn't steal anything." West scratched his jaw. "Is that about right?"

"What are you implying?" Astrid's blue eyes got icier. "Do you think I'm making things up? Lying?"

"No." He held up his hands. "Why would I think that? I saw everything with my own eyes."

"That's right. You did. I have no idea why this is happening." She dropped her chin to her chest and brushed off her jeans.

He studied the cascade of blond hair hiding her face and knew she was lying—not about the events. He did witness them. But he didn't believe for one minute she didn't have a clue about the motive for these…searches. Because that's exactly what it smelled like to him.

Somebody had searched Astrid's home and now her truck. Either the thief had found what he was looking for this time and Astrid had no intention of telling him what had been taken, or her assailant would look again.

Chase Thompson's dead body on the beach today had reminded West about the drug trade on this island. Was there more to Astrid Mitchell's fresh, outdoorsy mom persona?

Straightening up, she smoothed back her hair. "If there's nothing else, I'm going to head home."

"I'll follow you. You were able to get the broken window replaced?"

"My friend's stepson boarded it for me. I'm sure it will be fine. I'll make sure to arm the security system this time." She stepped over the glass and opened the door of her vehicle. "I don't really need an escort home."

"No problem. I'd rather follow you home than face the unpacked boxes at my place."

"I hear ya." She hopped into the truck and cranked on the engine. "Thanks for your help."

"Just doing my job." When he realized she didn't plan to wait for him to get into his car, he stepped back from the rumbling truck and strode to his vehicle.

Astrid followed all the rules of the road as he tailed her back to her luxury digs masquerading as a cabin. Once he verified she'd made it into the house safely, he backed down her drive and hit the main road.

On his way back to his boxes, West made a detour to the station. Astrid Mitchell exuded an air of mystery, and he wanted to get to the bottom of it to find out why her house and truck had been hit—at least that's what he told himself.

He'd start with her missing husband. He knew he could just ask around. Most likely every deputy working for him could give him the lowdown on Astrid Mitchell and her AWOL husband—but she'd find out about his curiosity, and he didn't want to give her a heads-up.

Seated behind his desk, he logged in to a couple of different databases, searching for a cop named Mitchell initially. His eyes glazed over as he scrolled through the findings. He knew it was a long shot when he started. He cleared that search and tapped his finger on the mouse.

Searching her name would be a better bet, as Astrid wasn't that common. Her real estate listings popped up first, and he perused a few of the houses. He was in a rental now, but if he stuck around, he'd buy something—and he'd use her as his agent. She could use the break.

As he skimmed down the screen, an article seemingly unrelated to Astrid caught his eye. His pulse jumped when he caught the drift of the story—a ring of dirty Seattle cops busted for drug dealing.

He clicked on the link and hunched forward to read the words on the screen. Several Seattle cops had been working in concert with a local drug dealer, Pierre Dumas, giving him a heads-up on busts and stealing drugs and money from raids. None of the cops had the name Mitchell. Why did a search on Astrid bring up this article?

He continued to read, and Astrid's name jumped out at him. Her ex-husband, Russ Crockett, was one of the dirty cops, and Astrid had testified against him. But before Crockett could be sentenced, he made a deal with the prosecution—names, dates, details—invaluable information for bringing down Dumas and his drug ring.

A quick phone call to a friend in high places gave West some insider information on Crockett. In exchange for his testimony, the Feds gave Crockett a new life in WITSEC. So Olly was right. His dad was hiding.

West leaned back in his chair and steepled his fingers. How much did Astrid know about her ex-husband's life? How much had she profited from his ill-gotten gains? Were the recent break-ins of Astrid's home and truck and the dead body on the beach all linked? Had Russ Crockett turned over all the drugs and money when the Feds arrested him? Or had he left some for safekeeping with his wife?

Olly's dad might be hiding, but was Olly's mom hiding something, too? If she was, West had every intention of finding out what that was—one way or another.

Chapter Five

Astrid studied her son spooning cereal into his mouth in front of Sam's TV, Peyton nowhere in sight. "Was he horrified when he discovered he'd had a sleepover with a girl?"

"He took it in stride, once I set that bowl of sugary breakfast food in front of him." Sam eyed her over the rim of her coffee cup. "Looks like his mom took getting conked on the head in stride, too. I'd be a nervous wreck if that happened to me, especially after the break-in."

Folding her arms across her chest, Astrid said, "I am a nervous wreck, but I don't want to telegraph that to Olly. I have no intention of telling him that someone attacked me. That's why I already got the truck window fixed."

"I get it, but you're so good at stuffing that all inside. I don't think I'd be able to pull it off. Peyton took one look at me after Bruce and I decided to separate and knew something was off." Sam sniffed and then took a quick sip of her brew to cover it.

"Yeah, well, I've had a lot of practice." Astrid patted the sore spot on the back of her head.

"I know you have, and I'm sorry." Sam squeezed Astrid's knee. "Do you think the two events from yesterday are related to Russ?"

Sam had lowered her voice and leaned in for the question, but Astrid slid a glance toward Olly anyway, still engrossed in SpongeBob. "I'm not sure. I mean, he's supposed to be secured away somewhere, starting a new life."

"I hope so, but do you think he'll ever give up on Olly?" Sam covered her mouth. "Sorry. I don't mean to give you more to worry about. Russ wouldn't dare pop his head up now. He's still in danger. Those people don't just forgive and forget."

Rubbing her chin, Astrid said, "That's exactly what concerns me."

The cartoon ended with Olly singing along to the theme song. Then he hopped up from the couch and twisted around. "Is it time to go, Mom?"

"Yes, it is. Thank your hosts before we leave." Astrid turned to Sam. "Thanks again."

"Don't thank me. If Anton and I had walked you to your truck, you never would've been…" Sam trailed off as Olly walked into the kitchen with two bowls, both half-filled with milk.

"I got Peyton's bowl, too." He put them in the sink, and Astrid's heart did a little dance.

"That's what I like to see."

Olly's face reddened to the roots of his blond hair, and his eyes widened. "Don't tell anyone, Mom."

"I swear, I won't." She drew a cross over her chest.

Sam held up her hand. "Peyton won't either. She'd be mortified."

"Mortified?" Olly tried out the word on his tongue.

"Embarrassed." Astrid tugged at his sleeve. "Get your sweatshirt."

Sam cupped her hand around her mouth and tilted her head back. "Peyton, say goodbye to your guest."

Peyton's voice carried down the stairs as she shrieked. "He's not my guest, Mom."

"Get down here, Peyton." Sam winked at Olly. "Told you."

With all the thanks and goodbyes out of the way and with Olly carrying a couple of slices of pizza wrapped in foil, Astrid followed him out to her truck. "That wasn't so bad, huh?"

Olly mumbled. "It was okay."

She jabbed him in the shoulder. "Admit it. You had fun."

Olly clambered into the truck and snapped his seat belt. "Yeah, Peyton's okay, but it's gonna be more fun at camp."

A flare of panic jumped in her breast. She didn't want to be away from Olly right now, but maybe he'd be safer in the woods with Porter Monroe and the rest of the Scouts than hanging around the house.

She forced her lips into a smile. "That's right. You need to pack up when we get home, so you're ready for pickup tonight. Remember what I told you."

"Stay with the group and follow the rules."

"Right on." She raised her fist for a bump, and Olly obliged.

Olly spent the rest of the ride home chattering about camp and all the activities lined up for them. Astrid made the appropriate noises at the right times, but her mind was jumping from the break-in at her house to the break-in of her truck.

The perpetrator hadn't stolen anything from either location. She'd bought the story about teens at the house getting spooked and dumping the drone in the trash, but that scenario didn't fly for the truck. She'd been assaulted.

She touched the back of her head and sucked in a breath

between her teeth. Maybe the person she'd surprised in her truck bed hadn't wanted to kill her, but he hadn't been afraid to take her down. Why? He could've just run off. She didn't have a chance at identifying him in his ski mask and gloves.

But perhaps he didn't want to take any chances. She slid a glance at Olly, describing how he planned to eat ten s'mores at the campfire. Anything bad that had ever happened in her life, except her brother's kidnapping twenty years ago, had been due to her association with her ex. Was this any different?

There had been speculation among law enforcement that Russ hadn't turned over all the drugs and money when he decided to rat out his buddies. The FBI had questioned her hard, but Russ had kept all of that from her. They weren't even married at the time, as the divorce had been finalized months before the testimony.

There was a good chance that Russ's associates didn't believe her. If anyone who had escaped the sting of the Dumas cartel, and there must've been a few, thought she had access to money and drugs, they wouldn't hesitate to track her down and force her to give it back. Was this just the beginning?

She flexed her sweaty hands on the steering wheel. She should've told West everything about her past instead of pretending she had no idea why someone would want to search her house and truck. She knew damned well why some criminal would want to toss the house of Russ Crockett's ex-wife.

By the time she pulled into the drive, Olly had grown silent. Had she missed her cue? She slid the truck into Park and turned her head toward him, giving him her full attention. "When we get inside, get your backpack and tell me what you want to wear. I'll do some laundry, and then we can get you packed up and ready to go."

With his chin at his chest, Olly rubbed the side of his thumb against the seam of his jeans. "Was there a dead guy at the cove?"

Astrid clamped her bottom lip between her teeth. It was impossible to keep anything from the kids on this island. "Where did you hear that?"

"Peyton told me. She heard it when she went into Mama Lucy's bedroom last night 'cuz she woke up and her mom wasn't home. She said her grandma was listening to something on her computer, and Peyton heard it."

"Yes, that's true. A guy walking his dog on the beach found the man's body." She squeezed her son's knee. "You don't have to worry about that. The police think it has something to do with drugs."

"When did the guy find him? Was he in the water or on the sand?"

Tilting her head, Astrid said, "He was discovered a little while before we got to Peyton's house. I don't know any of the details, but like I said, it was someone involved in drugs."

Had she blundered mentioning the drugs? How much had Olly known about his father's activities and why he'd had to go away?

"So, like, did the guy drown or something?"

Olly didn't even know the man had been murdered. She cut the engine and yanked the keys from the ignition. "Maybe he did. I'm not sure, Olly. Are you...concerned about it?"

"Nah." He shoved open the door and jumped to the ground. "Is my backpack in my closet?"

Before she had a chance to answer him, he was running toward the front door, clutching his pizza in front of him. She sighed. She was pretty sure the dead body at the cove would make its way into some scary campfire stories this week. Hopefully, Porter Monroe, the Scout leader, would have the good sense to steer the boys away from that and toward some good old-fashioned ghost stories.

She could handle the supernatural. It was the real-life monsters that scared her the most.

LATER THAT AFTERNOON, Logan Davidson's mother, Denise, shaded her eyes against the setting sun as she watched Olly and Logan hoist their gear into the back of her SUV. "I think it's easier this way. Have most of the boys in one pickup spot."

"Sure, sure. Makes sense to me." Of course Denise's place had to be the pickup spot. Denise was determined to be supermom, but Astrid was just as determined to get along with the mother of her son's best friend.

Crooking her finger at Olly, Astrid called. "You're not getting away without a hug."

Olly shrugged at Logan and then galloped back toward her, like a clumsy colt. He curled his arms around Astrid's waist and squeezed. "Be careful, Mom."

She hugged him tighter and patted him on the back. "That's my line. You don't have to worry about a couple of teenagers breaking into the house."

Wriggling out of her grasp, he stood on his tiptoes and planted a quick kiss on her cheek. "Bye."

"Have fun. Be careful. Love you."

He'd slammed the car door on her last words, and Denise chuckled. "Boys, huh? But I think we have it easier in the teen years than girl moms. I'm not looking forward to the arguments with Posey when she hits fourteen or fifteen."

Astrid didn't feel like opening the door to another soliloquy on the perfections of Posey Davidson, so she just nodded. "Thanks again for having the boys over, and call me if you need any help before the Scout leaders pick them up."

Denise chewed on her lip for a few seconds. "I'm kind of glad they're taking off this week. I hope the new sheriff makes an arrest in the Chase Thompson case before the boys come back. That one spooked Logan."

"It did?" Astrid raised her eyebrows. "Olly was asking questions about it, too. Do you think the kids were talking about it among themselves? Telling stories?"

"Not sure, but I hope it's not fodder for the campfire." Denise hoisted her purse onto her shoulder. "I'll talk to Porter about it before they leave."

"Thanks again, Denise."

Denise waved before ducking into the car, and Astrid kept waving until the car backed down the drive and disappeared.

She stayed on the porch, crossing her arms against the sudden chill. At least Olly wasn't the only kid worried about the dead body at the cove, so maybe his concern had nothing to do with his father's situation.

He also seemed more upset about the break-in than he'd let on. Why else tell her to be careful? He'd never said that to her before, and she hadn't even told him about the attack at her truck last night.

Releasing a long breath, she turned toward the house. She'd borrowed that drone from the office to get some aerial shots of a listing already on the market, and with Olly gone for the week, she'd better get to it tomorrow morning.

After the break-in, Astrid had secured the drone in Tate's safe. She probably should've put it in there when she brought it home the day before yesterday, but she hadn't anticipated anyone coming out here to break in at the precise time she'd forgotten to set the alarm.

She closed the door behind her and glanced at the security keypad on the wall. Had she forgotten to set it? That would be a rare mistake for her. She'd been security conscious ever since her separation from Russ a few years ago. Even though her brother didn't have cameras on the side door, the alarm would've gone off the minute someone smashed that window—if the security system had been armed.

She jogged upstairs and veered into the master suite, which Tate had made his own when he'd renovated this cabin. They'd all inherited a chunk of money from a wealthy uncle, and Tate had used his share to do a fantastic remodel of this cabin, which their parents had turned over to him. She hadn't minded being cut out. Tate's best friend had been kidnapped when they were children, and Tate had been traumatized. Her parents figured they owed him for that disruption of his childhood.

She ducked into his walk-in closet and knelt before the safe. Once she entered the combo, the heavy door swung open. The drone box dominated the space it shared with a few of Tate's weapons and some paperwork she ignored. She pulled it from the safe and locked up.

Clasping the box to her chest, she carried it downstairs and put it on the coffee table in the living room, where it had been when some thief decided to grab it. She hadn't had a chance to use it on any of her listings yet, but Davia

Reynolds, her boss at work, had assured her it was a breeze to use.

She opened the box and set the drone on the table while she fished for the instructions. She unfolded the little user manual and ran her finger along the small text on the glossy card. The agency planned to upgrade soon because this drone was already out of date—no live feeds, no video going straight to your phone or computer. This one used a physical memory card, but it still seemed high-tech to her.

As she read through the instructions, she located all the parts and buttons and switches. She assumed the drone had a memory card installed, but she couldn't open the slot and didn't want to push it.

When she felt ready, she grabbed a sweatshirt and carried the drone outside. She'd do a test run here before taking it out to the property, and she had about fifteen minutes before it got dark.

Standing in front of the cabin, she set the power and tried to launch the drone. It buzzed but didn't take flight. She set it beside her on the porch while she perused the directions again but no luck.

She knew Davia planned to meet some clients tonight in the office, so Astrid shot off a text to her boss, who'd used the drone before. If she could get some pointers tonight, she'd be ready to go tomorrow.

Davia replied that she'd be in the office for the next thirty minutes and would be happy to help Astrid with the drone.

Astrid made it to the office with time to spare, pulling into a space next to an SUV belonging to the Dead Falls Island Sheriff's Department. Davia hadn't mentioned that her client was a cop.

As Astrid approached the office, her step hitched as she

caught sight of Sheriff West Chandler talking to Davia, looking almost as sexy in his civilian clothes as he did in uniform. He should've told her he was looking to buy, so she could represent him. Maybe he'd decided to steer clear of her and her messy life.

Squaring her shoulders, she pushed through the door. "Hi, Davia. Glad I caught you. Hello, Sheriff."

"I was just showing my other clients out when Sheriff Chandler showed up." Davia's gaze darted from West to Astrid. "He's interested in seeing a few properties, and he requested you as his agent. Said he already talked to you."

"That's right." She nodded at West. They'd sort of talked, but he hadn't seemed to be in the market immediately. But she'd take the business. "Be happy to help."

West said, "Now I'm even more satisfied with my choice of real estate brokers. You're obviously motivated, to be working after hours."

"Don't get used to it." Astrid patted the box. "I'm just here to get some last-minute instruction from Davia on using the drone."

As West raised his eyebrows and cleared his throat, Astrid held her breath. She willed him with her death stare not to mention the almost-theft of the drone. She hadn't told Davia and didn't want to mention it—not yet.

"Okay, let's see what you're doing." Davia cleared a space on her desk and patted it.

Astrid pulled the drone from the box and placed it on the blotter gently, as if it hadn't already been through hell. "I set this. Turned on this switch and checked that this was on. No go."

Davia squinted at the drone and tapped its side. "No wonder it won't work. It's broken."

"Broken?" Astrid's heart jumped. "How can that be? You showed me how it worked before boxing it and letting me take it home the other night. It seemed okay then."

"You haven't tried to use it yet?" Davia wrinkled her nose at the drone perched on her desk.

"No. I mean, just a half hour ago when I tried to give it a test run. But I didn't break anything. It never made it off the ground."

Davia flicked a finger at the silent machine on her desk. "Between the time I gave it to you and the time you set it up for a test, someone used it. Someone launched it, and it looks like someone tried to bat it out of the sky."

Chapter Six

Astrid's face drained of all color, and her blue eyes widened. "That's not possible. I haven't tried it yet."

West bit the inside of his cheek. He'd kept mum earlier when it became clear that Astrid hadn't told her boss about the near-miss theft of the drone. He wasn't here to call anyone out, but this shed a different light on things. Had someone damaged the drone when they tossed it in the trash? Or maybe they damaged it before and that's *why* they tossed it in the trash.

Davia screwed up one side of her mouth. "Could you have dropped it in transit?"

"Dropped it?" Astrid twisted her fingers in front of her. "No, b-but someone took it from my house and dumped it my trash can."

"Oh." Davia's mouth remained in an *O* after she uttered the word.

Spreading her hands, Astrid said, "I know. I'm sorry. I…we just thought it was some teens who broke in, saw the drone, snatched it and then thought better of it."

"Do you think they might've had time to take it up?" Davia tapped her scarlet fingernails against the drone's gray body. "Even though I mentioned before that it could've been dropped, it really looks like someone smacked it."

West peered over Davia's shoulder and followed the path of her fingers. If you weren't familiar with the drone, you might miss the indentations on its side. He reached around her and poked at a flat button. "What's that? It looks bent."

"That's the button for the memory card slot. This drone is an old one that we were planning to replace anyway for one that does a live video feed to a phone or computer." She wedged her finger against the button. "Seems stuck."

Astrid dropped to the chair next to Davia's desk. "I'm so sorry, Davia. I don't know how that could've happened. I can't imagine how the thieves had time to fly the drone, wreck it, and then stuff it back in the box and in my trash can."

"Don't worry about it. This is a good excuse to fast-track that replacement." Davia pulled on her earlobe, rotating the diamond stud embedded there. "Look, I know Olly is a good kid and mine were, too, but they were no angels. Now that they're adults, they tell me all kinds of things they got up to—things I'd rather not know about. Do you think…?"

Davia left her words hanging, and Astrid wedged her fingers against her bottom lip. "Olly? You think Olly might have flown the drone?"

Waving her hands in the air, Davia said, "Just a thought, but boys, drones." She shrugged. "It's an irresistible combo. It's not a big deal, Astrid. The thing was on its last legs, anyway. I can tell corporate it finally crashed and burned, and we need that new one if they want us to stay on top of things out here—literally. A lot of the properties on this island need those bird's-eye view pictures for a sale. I gotta go. My hubby was irked enough that I stayed a little late for those clients on our date night. Can you lock up?"

"Sure, I have my keys." Astrid patted her purse hanging at her side. "I can pay to have it fixed, whether it was Olly or not. It was damaged under my care."

Davia flicked the drone with her finger. "It might be reparable, but don't knock yourself out. And go easy on Olly. The kid's had it rough."

West turned his head and pretended to inspect the drone as Astrid put her hand to her heart. "Thanks, Davia. I might still see about getting it fixed because I wanted to use it for my listing in Misty Hollow."

"You're gonna need all the help you can get with that property." Davia gave an exaggerated shiver. "Full disclosure, right?"

"I have it drawn up for the contract already. It's still a great piece of land—despite its history."

"Thanks for dropping by, Sheriff. Maybe you should try to sell Sheriff Chandler the Misty Hollow property." Davia winked at Astrid. "At least he might not be spooked."

When Davia swept out the door on a cloud of floral perfume, Astrid slumped against the back of the love seat. "I never thought of Olly. He was acting kind of weird that day. I thought he'd be more freaked out by the break-in. And then he was the one who conveniently found the drone in the trash."

West perched on the arm of the love seat next to her and crossed his arms. "When would he have had time to mess with the drone? Wasn't he at the Spring Fling with you? Didn't he come home with you where you discovered the theft together?"

"He wasn't with me at the Fling all day. I dropped him and his bike off at his best friend's house. They were riding their bikes most of the day, and then his friend's mother dropped them off at the Fling."

"Then how'd he get the drone?"

Her hand brushed his thigh as she raised her it to drag through her blond locks. "I *thought* I set the security system when we left that morning."

"What does that mean?" He shifted his leg, still tingling from her unintended contact.

"It means Olly and Logan could've ridden their bikes back to the house, used the key to get in and take the drone. Then Olly forgot to arm the system when he left." She smacked her hand on the cushion beside her. "That little sneak."

"Wait." He hopped up from the love seat and picked up the drone from Davia's desk. "Why'd he leave it in the trash, and why'd he break the window if he had a key?"

She drummed her fingers on the arm of the love seat he'd just vacated. "Not sure, but maybe when he returned with the drone, he remembered the camera at the front, so he went around to the side door. At that point, he could've seen the broken window, freaked out and stashed the drone in the trash to be collected at a later time. Or he and Logan could've broken the window by accident, got spooked and dumped the drone."

"You said the camera wouldn't work without the security system set."

She lifted her shoulders. "Either Olly never knew that, forgot or he believed he set the alarm when he left after taking the drone. Anything could be going through that kid's head. It has to be the one of those explanations. The drone was not broken when I checked it out of the office. I don't think a couple of thieves would've had the time or inclination to launch it."

"I don't know about that. We can't rule it out. Can you talk to Olly about it?"

"Not right now. He's on a Scout camping trip for the rest of the week. He'll be back before Easter." She bounded from the love seat and joined him at the desk. "If Olly or someone else launched the drone, we should be able to check that data card for the footage. That might tell us something."

"Except—" West tapped the side of the drone "—the damage to the drone affected the slot for the card. We can't get it out."

"Unless I can find someone to fix it. That might solve the mystery." She reached across him to stuff the drone back in the box, and her hair tickled the back of his hand. "I think I know someone who can handle the job."

"Right now?"

She checked her phone. "If I can catch him before he leaves his shop. He's actually an auto mechanic, but he knows his electronics and can fix anything. I mean, unless it's a software issue."

"I think it's definitely mechanical, and even if he can't fix the thing, maybe he can pop that sleeve open without doing further damage so you can retrieve the video card and find out where it was used last. That should be able to tell you if Olly or someone else flew it."

Astrid pulled her phone from her purse and tapped the display. A few seconds later, she gave him a thumbs-up. "Hi, Alexa. Is Jimmy still around? I have a job for him."

She cocked her head and listened before speaking again. "It's a drone. Can he look at it? I'll rush it right over before you guys close up shop for the day."

While Astrid finished her call, West packaged the drone back in the box. Even if Olly did take the drone out for a test drive and break the window on the kitchen door, it didn't explain the attack on Astrid last night. Something felt off to him.

"Okay." Astrid dusted her hands together. "Jimmy will have a look at it. The garage is still open, so I'll drop it off on my way home."

"Do you have plans for dinner?" Astrid's face showed as much surprise as he hoped he was hiding on his own face. That invitation came out of left field even if he did need more from this woman—more information, more conversation. "I was thinking we could grab a bite, and then you could show me this property at Misty Hollow."

"Are you serious?"

He patted his stomach. "About dinner? Hell, yeah. I'm starving."

"About the property at Misty Hollow." She wedged her hip against the edge of the desk and blinked. "Do you know the history of the place? Did you hear me and Davia talk about the disclosures?"

"Now, what kind of new sheriff would I be if I didn't familiarize myself with the crime on this island—current and past? I know all about the massacre committed by the foster son Brian Lamar aka Addison Abbott at that property thirty years ago."

"It doesn't scare you off?" A little smile touched the corner of her mouth.

"Brain Lamar is dead. Are you saying the place is haunted or doomed or something?"

Lifting one shoulder, she said, "Just figured it would be a tough sale. That's why I really, really wanted to use the drone. It's a fabulous space—despite its macabre history."

"I'd like to see it—after dinner." West's interest in the property wasn't completely sincere. He just figured he needed a cover for randomly inviting Astrid out for dinner. Might as well pretend it was business-related.

"It's going to be dark by then." She peeked out the window. "It's already dark."

"Best time to view a haunted property, wouldn't you say?"

"As long as I'm with the sheriff." Hunching her shoulders, she hugged herself. "That place is spooky."

"Then we'd better get going. You have any suggestions for dinner?" His gaze flickered over her casual outfit of jeans, running shoes and a hoodie. She looked fresh and pretty, but she'd look good in a potato sack.

"Pizza? We still might get a seat at Luigi's. A lot of families are off the island for spring break. Also, it's down the street from Jimmy's garage."

"Sounds perfect. I hate to admit that I've already been to Luigi's twice since I got to the island."

"No shame in craving a good pizza." She dangled her key chain. "I'll lock up and meet you there, after dropping off the drone."

He glanced out the window at the darkening sky. "I'll wait and follow you over to Jimmy's."

"Not necessary, but okay."

Something in his gut told him it *was* necessary, not that he could be Astrid Mitchell's bodyguard 24/7. He stood outside while Astrid locked up a few drawers and then secured the front door. When he walked her to her truck, he asked, "I didn't see your report today on the attack. Was there anything missing from your truck?"

"The lock on the toolbox was broken, and I searched through those tools in there, but I couldn't tell if anything was missing. My brother stashes some of his tools in my truck, so I'll have to ask him."

He held the door open for her as she hopped onto the driver's seat. "Have you checked with him about any possible missing items from the house?"

"Nope." She shook her head from side to side. "Not yet."

"You're avoiding it."

Resting her elbows on the steering wheel, she said, "My brother is a worrier. You have no idea. I don't want to set him off while he's busy in DC. The tools don't matter. I doubt he had anything of value in my truck."

"Does he have anything to worry about?" He curled his fingers around the edge of the door.

"If he doesn't, he'll find something." She grabbed the door handle of the truck and tugged. "Let's go."

West released the door, and she slammed it. Was that her way of telling him to mind his own business? As sheriff, her business *was* his business.

He followed her for a short ten-minute drive to Jimmy's Auto at the end of the main drag through town. He parked next to her and got out of his car. Might as well get to know as many residents of the island as possible. Also, if Jimmy looked at the drone and figured he couldn't fix it, they might as well force open the cover to the memory card slot and retrieve it and just hope they didn't damage anything.

The rolling door on the garage, securely closed, gleamed in the lights above it, which spilled onto a few cars parked on the side. A cheery glow emanated from the front office, though, and he could see two figures through the window.

Astrid marched to the door, oblivious of him on her heels. She almost let the door swing closed in his face, but he caught it, and she jumped.

"I didn't know you were coming inside."

"Thought I should meet Jimmy and his wife. I understand he works on our vehicles."

She searched his face for minute, as if not sure she could trust him. If she couldn't trust the new sheriff in town, who could she trust? He'd have to work on that. He used to be so good at inspiring trust in people—until he'd lost all that good faith with one action.

At the sound of a woman's voice from the back, Astrid looked away quickly. "Hey, Alexa. Thanks for waiting."

"Jimmy had to wrap up, anyway. Hello, Sheriff Chandler. I'm Jimmy's wife, Alexa Galvin."

He shook hands with the petite, dark-haired woman across the scarred counter, bearing stickers from oil and tire brands. "Good to meet you."

Jimmy came from the back and held up his clean hands before extending one to West. "You here to take a look at those contracts we have with the city for the vehicles?"

"If you have them."

"Alexa, hon, can you grab those for the sheriff while I take a look at Astrid's drone?"

A minute later, West had to drag his attention away from Astrid's conversation with Jimmy, as Alexa plopped some folders on the counter in front of him. "You can take these, Sheriff, as long as you return them."

"Absolutely." West grabbed the files from the glass top with no intention of reviewing them. He didn't even know if maintaining these contracts fell under his purview and not the city council's.

As he tucked the folders under his arm, Astrid smiled at him and clapped her hands. "Jimmy thinks he can fix it."

"Don't get too excited, Astrid." Jimmy ran a hand over his shaved head. "I'll have a look, but at least I can get that memory card out for you without breaking the whole thing and ruining it."

"I appreciate it, Jimmy."

West and Astrid left the Galvins to close up shop and meandered back to their cars.

West jerked his thumb to the side. "Walking distance."

"Yeah, that'll come in handy after we stuff our faces with pizza." Astrid patted her flat stomach.

He kept his mouth shut, but willowy Astrid didn't look like she needed to worry about working off calories.

They fell into step together as they walked to Luigi's, a bustling pizza place that catered to both seated diners and takeout. He knew all about the takeout.

His mouth watered as they stepped inside, and the scent of garlic curled around him. He'd been an oddball in Chicago, preferring a thin-crust pie to the deep-dish delicacy served throughout Chi-town—as if he needed another reason to abandon that city.

Standing on her tiptoes, even though she was probably one of the tallest people in the restaurant, Astrid surveyed the room. "Do you want to grab one of those tables, and I'll order at the counter?"

"Let's switch that around. You find a good table, and I'll place our order. Just let me know what you want."

"Pepperoni is fine with me and a glass of house red."

"Got it." He pivoted toward the counter and waited in a short line, as people threw curious glances his way. A buddy of his who'd left the Chicago PD a few years before he did and settled in as a small-town sheriff in Colorado had advised him to get to know as many people as possible on a personal level. Eat out in the local restaurants, shop locally, use local service people—see and be seen. West had known being the sheriff of an island department like Dead Falls would involve a lot of PR and people-pleasing. He couldn't complain about it now.

The young man at the counter adjusted his Luigi's pizza cap when West stepped up to the register. "Hey, Sheriff. What can we get you tonight? You plan on trying every combo we got?"

"Just about—" West zeroed in on the guy's name tag "—Evan, but tonight I just need a large pepperoni, a glass of your house red and a…soda."

He'd have to check with his friend on the rules for drinking alcohol in public. He was off the clock and in civvies, but was a small-town sheriff ever off the clock? He'd technically been off duty last night when Astrid had been attacked, even though he'd been questioning people in the Salty Crab about the Chase Thompson murder.

Evan took his order, handed him a plastic cup for the self-serve soda machine and gave him a number for his table. "The wine will be right out, Sheriff."

West nodded, aware of a few side-eye glances, and he wanted to say aloud the wine wasn't for him. He snatched up his cup and edged over to the soda machine. He'd probably never feel comfortable drinking in front of the good citizens of Dead Falls.

He joined Astrid at the table by the window and set down his drink next to the water glasses. "Mission accomplished. Wine's on the way."

"I guess I should make a full confession here."

His gaze jumped to her face as his hand jerked, the soda fizzing and the ice clinking in protest. Did she have something else to tell him about the drone? The break-in? Her ex-husband? "Oh?"

Leaning in close, she cupped a hand around her mouth. "I just had Luigi's pepperoni pizza last night."

He blinked and sucked down some soda. "I won't tell anyone. I'm the sheriff. I'm trustworthy."

The smile on her lips wobbled. "Those two statements could totally be mutually exclusive."

Before he could start down the path that might lead to a discussion of her ex, a young woman arrived with the wine. "Red wine?"

Astrid raised her hand, and the woman placed it on the table. "Enjoy."

Tilting the glass toward him, Astrid asked, "Should we toast to the drone's recovery? Or your arrival in town?"

"How about both?" He tapped his cup to hers and shoved the straw into his mouth.

As she sipped her wine, her eyes widened over the rim. "Look who followed us over here."

He turned his head toward the entrance and spotted Jimmy and Alexa from the garage waiting in the takeout line. Jimmy's eyes met his, and they nodded.

West asked, "Did Jimmy seem confident he could fix the drone?"

"Let's just say he was cautiously optimistic, but at least I trust him to pop out that memory card without destroying it. I don't know what that will solve, exactly, but maybe I can have some peace of mind that nobody actually broke into the house and that Olly caused the damage—if that's peace of mind."

"Except—" West toyed with his straw "—someone at-tacked you at your truck."

She swirled her wine before taking a sip. "Could be unrelated."

From the corner of his eye, he noticed someone charging toward their table. His muscles tensed and then relaxed when he saw Jimmy approaching them. West said, "Great minds think alike."

"Sorry to bother you, Sheriff. I know you're off duty and all, but I just got a notification on my phone that the security at my shop was breached. If you don't wanna come, that's okay, but I thought since you're already sitting here, and we were just at the shop…"

As the hair on the back of his neck stood at attention, West exchanged a quick glance with Astrid. "Of course I'll come. Astrid, can you stay for the food?"

"No way. I'm coming, too." She grabbed her purse and pointed at the waitress, who'd brought the wine. "Taylor, can you box up our order? We'll be back to pick it up later."

"Sure." Taylor's brown eyes sparkled as her gaze bounced between Jimmy and West. Probably hoping for all the details when they came back for the pizza.

The Galvins had driven from their shop to Luigi's, and Jimmy waved them into the back seat of the car, where West's knees almost hit his chin. "What kind of security system do you have, Jimmy?"

"Camera, alarm, the whole shebang." He pounded a fist on the steering wheel. "I hope all they took was petty cash. I can't afford to lose my tools. Can't do business without my tools."

West asked, "Did you see any camera footage on your phone?"

"It's not live. I can look at it later, but all I got on my phone was the alarm indicating a break-in."

"When we get there, let me go first in case someone's still hanging around." West felt for the weapon beneath his bulky flannel shirt.

Jimmy pulled up to the shop with the alarm blasting

into the night. West doubted any thief would stick around through this noise, but he ordered everyone to stay in the car.

He jumped out, his hand hovering over his gun at his waist. He yelled, "Police! Come out with your hands up."

With the toe of his shoe, he nudged the door with the shattered glass. It didn't budge, so he yanked the sleeve of his shirt over his hand and pulled open the door, the loose glass tinkling to the ground.

The lights had gone on as part of the alarm, and West stepped into the shop's office. He squeezed behind the counter, noting the closed register. Didn't mean they didn't open it and take the cash. Jimmy and Alexa would have to check that.

He was more interested in the drone. He and Astrid had had the same thought the minute Jimmy reported the break-in.

"All clear?" Jimmy called out as his work boots crunched the broken glass at the entrance to the shop.

"Yeah, don't touch anything, though." West turned toward Jimmy, Astrid hovering behind him. "Hey, did you leave Astrid's drone in the office?"

"You're kidding me." Jimmy stormed into the office, past West to a workbench between the office and the garage. He smacked the workbench, and all the tools rattled.

"Damn! Astrid, I'm sorry. Someone stole your drone."

Chapter Seven

The world tilted for Astrid, and she grabbed the corner of the counter. What the hell was going on? Why did someone want that drone so badly, and how'd they know she'd brought it here?

She glanced over her shoulder at Alexa still sitting in the car, her face pinched, and then into the darkness beyond the small parking lot. Had someone followed her from the office? That meant whoever took the drone knew where she worked.

Russ knew where she worked. Did Russ's former associates know?

Jimmy looked up from the register and shrugged. "They didn't take the petty cash."

"Check your tools in the garage, Jimmy." West pointed at the door between the office and the work area.

Cocking his head, Jimmy scratched his chin. "Doesn't look like they got as far as the garage. The door's still locked, and nothing looks broken, unlike my front door."

"Have a look anyway to be sure. You got a pair of gloves to put on?"

Jimmy used a pen to open a desk drawer. "Alexa keeps a stash because she doesn't like touching anything with grease on it. I told her she's in the wrong business."

With a pair of blue gloves on his hands, Jimmy eased open the door to the garage and elbowed on the lights. He called over his shoulder. "At least the cars are still here."

As the door closed behind him, Astrid spun around to face West. "Someone broke in here to steal that drone."

"Looks like it." He dragged a hand through his dark brown hair. "Could it just be someone who wants a drone and knows you have this one? It's not like there's a handy drone shop in town where someone could buy one."

Astrid sawed her bottom lip with her teeth. "Someone is that desperate for a drone that they'd break into my house, follow me from work and then break into Jimmy's Auto?"

"And search your truck and assault you when you caught him in the act. Not to mention, he had the drone and dumped it."

Lifting her shoulders, she spread her hands wide. "Doesn't seem plausible, does it? But I don't know what else is plausible. I guess now that he has the drone, even though it's broken, maybe he'll stop harassing me and anyone else who has it."

"Maybe it's not the drone he wants but whatever it recorded." West narrowed his eyes. "Who had the drone before you?"

"Not sure. There are only three of us in this Discovery Bay office." She held up three fingers. "Me, Davia and Sumit Rao. I can call and ask them, but Davia seemed pretty sure the drone had been launched after I picked it up. Maybe the thieves took it from my house and did fly it. Then they dumped it in the trash and are worried we can use the footage to track them down."

"Okay." West put his finger to his lips as Jimmy came in from the garage.

"Nope. Nothing." Jimmy tugged on the bill of his Seahawks cap, the blue glove still encasing his hand. "Whoever it was broke my window, snatched your drone and took off. Last laugh on him, man. Guess he didn't know you took the drone here for repair."

"I guess not." Astrid pointed to the smashed window. "I know a guy who can board that up for you tonight."

Jimmy lifted up his hands, showing both sides. "I can do that myself. I'll just have Alexa go back to Luigi's for our pizza while I work on it."

West said, "I can get someone to come out here first thing in the morning to check for prints. My guess is you're going to have a lot of prints on these doors."

"I'm sure we are, Sheriff, but I appreciate the effort." Jimmy shook his head at Astrid. "I'm real sorry about that drone, Astrid. I can include it when I file a claim for my broken window."

"I'll ask Davia, but I don't think that's necessary, Jimmy." She gestured outside to Alexa, who hadn't budged from the passenger seat of the car. "Should we tell Alexa to go ahead and pick up the pizza and meet you back here?"

"Could you? She can give you a lift back to Luigi's. Sorry I interrupted your dinner, but I guess it's good that you know the drone was stolen."

"Yeah, great." Astrid raised her brows at West. "Do you want to go back to Luigi's with Alexa to grab our pizza or just call it a night?"

"Call it a night? I'm still starving." West patted his stomach, flat beneath his T-shirt, visible now that he'd unbuttoned his flannel shirt to get to his weapon.

She should've known he'd be carrying, but now she felt

even safer in his presence. Of course, Russ was always packing, and that hadn't made her feel safe at all.

"Okay, but I'd rather we just drive our cars the few blocks to Luigi's. No offense, Jimmy, but I don't feel like leaving it in front of your shop."

"I don't blame you." He hitched up his beefy shoulders.

Astrid delivered Jimmy's message to Alexa, after assuring her nothing in the shop had been stolen except her drone, and then she and West hopped into their own cars and drove back to Luigi's.

After she parked, she joined West on the sidewalk where he waited for her. As he reached for the door of the restaurant, Astrid said, "I don't really need more pizza. You can take the whole thing, and I'll eat some leftovers I have at home."

Stepping in after her, he said, "Did you forget about the second part of this...outing? You were going to show me the Misty Hollow property by the light of the moon. Now we have moonlight *and* pizza. Maybe we can make a pizza offering to the ghosts and ghouls who show up."

Butterflies swirled in her stomach. Had he been about to call this a date? Weird, how all their so-called dates so far involved break-ins and assaults.

She waved at Alexa, two ahead of them in the takeout line, and said to West, "You're serious about looking at that property tonight."

"Unless you'd rather not." He pulled the receipt for their food out of his pocket. "Then I'll take my half of the pizza and head back to my rental."

"The customer is always right, or at least almost always, but there's no way I'd let you put an offer on that property without seeing it in the daylight."

"No way I ever would." He smacked his receipt on the counter and turned toward the teenager taking orders. "We had to leave in a hurry, and…"

Astrid supplied the name. "Taylor. I asked Taylor to box it up for us, Reggie."

"Oh, right." He wagged his pen at them. "Large pepperoni, right."

"That's right." She stopped Reggie as he started to turn toward a counter behind him stacked with pizza boxes. "Can you throw in some paper plates and napkins?"

"Sure will." Reggie gathered their order, piled it on the counter and grabbed a couple bottles of water out of the fridge. "These are on the house for keeping our community safe, Sheriff Chandler."

"Wow, thanks." Two spots of color formed on West's cheeks, and Astrid nudged him as they carried their food outside.

"Reggie's gesture embarrassed you?"

"In Chicago, kids his age are more likely to spit on you." His jaw tightened.

Was that why he'd left the big city for a small-town job? West didn't seem like the type of cop that would be sensitive about his PR, but maybe that's why he settled here.

She stumbled to a stop when she reached her truck. "Should we go separately? You can follow me. My place is located closer to Misty Hollow than town, and I'd hate for you to have to drive all the way back here to drop me off, and I wouldn't want to do it for you, either. If we each take our own vehicles, we can peel off from Misty Hollow after the séance."

He chuckled. "I didn't agree to any séance, but I'll follow you over. Can I take the food in my car so I can have a slice on the drive there? I wasn't kidding about my imminent starvation."

She plopped the bag with plates and napkins on top of the pizza box in his arms. "Of course, but I'm taking one of the waters with me."

A few minutes later as she pulled onto the main road that almost made a circle around the island, she glanced in her rearview mirror to make sure West was following her. Could she really put this drone mishap behind her? Davia wasn't too upset about it, and if the thief got what he wanted from Jimmy's Auto, he'd leave her alone. At this point, she didn't care who took the drone and what he… or she…filmed with it.

But why had this person left it in her trash can in the first place and why so desperate to get it back now?

She planned to make a call to the Scout leaders tonight to check up on Olly. The kids weren't allowed to bring their phones but if they were feeling homesick, they could talk to their parents. Should she question him about the drone and ruin his camping trip?

As she approached the waterfall, she flicked on her wipers and her turn signal. West's indicator light mimicked her own, letting her know he'd seen her direction. She headed across the bridge, the falls to her right, creating a white cascade in the darkness and a silent roar through her closed windows.

When she reached the other side of the water, she turned left onto the road that curved around the river through Misty Hollow. No new subdivision existed out this way, and only a few vacation cabins dotted the landscape. Beyond Misty Hollow, the Samish Reservation sprawled through the forest.

But between the falls and Samish land lay the property of Shannon Toomey, the niece of the man who'd been slaughtered here, along with his entire family, by his preteen foster child, Addison Abbott. Terrible story. Great property. Possible client.

She switched on her high beams as she approached the Keldorf property, the light sweeping over the burned-out husk of the barn. She'd suggested her client tear down the barn, at least, but Shannon refused to do anything to the property she'd inherited from her father, murdered by the same person who killed her uncle. Not surprising she didn't want to set foot on the place.

She parked her truck, leaving her headlights glowing, and West pulled up beside her, his lights joining hers. When he exited his vehicle with a flashlight in his hand, she raised both hands to her face.

"Are you seriously expecting a tour by flashlight?"

"I'm assuming there's no electricity, so, yeah." He aimed the beam at the barn. "Should we start there?"

"There is no there. It's a burned-out barn, nothing left inside."

"I'd like to check it out." He scanned the light back and forth around the charred barn, and the flickers almost looked like flames racing across the wood again. "It's part of the history of the property. I read the PI and child psychologist who broke the case were in here when Brian Lamar aka Addison Abbott tossed in a Molotov cocktail."

She wedged a hand on her hip. "You really do know your Dead Falls crime history."

"Shall we?" He cupped her elbow with his hand, the flashlight in his other hand leading their way toward the barn.

Astrid's shoes crunched the ground beneath as she squared her shoulders. She didn't need West's assistance to reach the hulking ruin, but she'd take it.

The firefighters had hacked through the barn door, leaving a gaping hole that looked like a screaming mouth.

Astrid shook her head. Fanciful musings. She'd better get her head on straight about this property if she hoped to sell it. She doubted West's commitment to the property. He'd just wanted to…what? Get her alone?

She of all people knew you couldn't trust a cop just because he was a cop—or a sheriff.

West ducked into the opening and whistled. "This place is small. Imagine being trapped in here with a raging fire."

"That PI and child psychologist are friends of mine." She shivered. "I couldn't believe it when it happened. I keep telling the owner, Shannon Toomey, to knock this down."

"Would she mind if you got someone to do it for her? Maybe she just doesn't want to deal with it but would be okay if someone made all the plans for her."

"Maybe." Astrid pivoted and flung her hand toward the house, another eyesore. "I can't imagine the buyer keeping any of this. People died in that house…children."

West spun her around and planted his hands on her shoulders. "You head back to your truck. I'll check out the house on my own, and then we'll eat some pizza overlooking the waterfall."

With his flashlight pointed at the ground, the moonlight illuminated his strong features. In this aspect, it looked as if he could take on just about anything—including ghosts.

She dug her heels in the ground. "I'm the Realtor here. I'll show you around."

It didn't take long to show West the main house. He poked his head into the rooms, empty and devoid of furniture now. Someone had even taken the cages where Mr. Keldorf had kept his finches. Addison Abbott had killed the birds, too.

When he'd seen enough, they stepped outside and Astrid locked up the front door, a replacement for the one that had been hanging on its hinges.

She brushed her hands together. "You've seen the worst of it now. Wait until you see the land in the light of day. That's what I was hoping to showcase with the drone footage."

"Maybe Davia will buy a replacement sooner rather than later. She didn't seem too eager for you to get the old one repaired."

"No, she didn't." Astrid patted her rumbling stomach. "I'm hungry. Do you want to follow me to the lookout over the falls? We can sit in the back of my truck and feast… on the pizza."

"Lead the way."

She practically sprinted to her vehicle. Why was she such a sucker for men in uniforms? West wasn't even wearing his tonight, and she was still flirting with him.

She'd put it down to her relief over the drone. She hadn't been thrilled that someone had broken into Jimmy's shop, but at least her intruder had gotten what he wanted. What did she care if someone snatched that drone, launched it and broken it? If they were that distressed about getting it back, let them have it and leave her alone.

Cranking on the engine of her truck, she waved out the window to West. His headlights trailed after her as she headed back onto the road. Before crossing the bridge, she turned left toward the falls and backed her truck into the overlook.

As she lowered the tailgate on the truck bed, West pulled up beside her. She retrieved the pizza from the cab of his truck, and West scrambled from his SUV with a blanket under his arm.

"Might as well be comfortable." He shook out the blanket and spread it over the truck bed. Then he turned and took the pizza and plastic bag from her.

As she hoisted herself into the truck bed, he hunched forward to help her, putting one hand under her arm. Then he crawled toward the cab and patted the blanket beside him. "I already had a slice, so you get first dibs on the pizza. Is it good cold?"

Placing her hand on top of the box, she said, "Let's call it lukewarm."

He dug into the plastic bag for some plates and napkins, pulling out a bottle of water, too. He settled his back against the cab and stretched his long, denim-clad legs in front of him, crossing them at the ankles.

With the box flipped open on her lap, she tore off two pieces of pizza and dropped them onto a paper plate. Sliding the box onto his thighs, she said, "Your turn."

"The falls are beautiful at night." He waved his slice in the direction of the water cascading in a sheer drop from the cliffs above it. "You ever go in the caves behind it?"

"When I was younger." She took a sip of water from her bottle. "Most of the teens on this island make that pilgrimage. I know Olly will do it one day, and I shudder to think about it. If you venture too far out of the caves, the rock is slippery with algae. One wrong move..."

West chewed, his eyes narrowing. "Not to mention a few suicides and murders."

"Exactly." She wiped her greasy fingers on a napkin. "That's the problem with this island. Great beauty can mask great danger—or evil."

"In the big city, you don't even get the benefit of nature's beauty—just the cold, hard, nasty truth." He ripped off another bite of pizza with his teeth, and she shot him a side glance.

He seemed easygoing enough, but sometimes a sliver of anger or anxiety peeked through the nice-guy sheriff veneer. He'd moved to Discovery Bay from Chicago for a reason, but she didn't really want to hear those reasons.

That sat in silence for several minutes, eating and watching the waterfall, her shoulder occasionally brushing against his as she reached for her water. She hadn't spent a night like this with a man in a long time. And maybe it meant nothing to him, but it felt like a small patch on her heart.

She jumped when his phone rang, placing her hand on her chest. Trouble on the island would follow him everywhere. Sheriff Hopkins, West's predecessor, didn't let it faze him or change his lifestyle. He always had other deputies handle the calls and the people of the island while he glad-handed with the Discovery Bay mayor, council and developers.

When West finished murmuring into the phone, he brushed off the thighs of his jeans. "Little trouble out by the trailer park. Hope you don't mind, but I feel as if I need to poke my nose into every situation at this stage of the game."

"I get it. Thanks for suggesting this. It was a nice break."

She pointed at the pizza. "I insist you take the rest home. Like I told you, I had Luigi's last night and with Olly gone, I can't handle the leftovers."

"You don't have to twist my arm." He got to his knees and folded the paper plates before stuffing them in the plastic bag and dropping their napkins in after the plates. "I'll take the trash with me and get rid of it on the way."

"You don't have to twist *my* arm." She dusted crumbs from her hands over the edge of the truck bed and gripped the sides to push to her feet.

West hopped out of the truck first. Holding the pizza box in one hand, he extended his other to help her down.

She accepted the support and jumped to the ground. He kept hold of her hand a few seconds after she'd gained purchase on the gravel and gave her fingers a slight squeeze. Or had she imagined that?

"Thanks for coming out to the property to take my mind off that damned drone. I know you're not really interested in the Misty Hollow murder house."

"You never know." He winked. "I'm a believer in new beginnings. I have to be."

Gathering her hair with one hand, she tilted her head. "I think we all have to be."

He slammed her tailgate, and the sound echoed over the water. "You're okay to get home by yourself?"

She snorted. "I grew up here, Sheriff. You should be asking yourself that question. It's dark out by the trailer park."

"Yeah, I have a surefire GPS in my car. Thanks for the tour, Astrid." His eyes seemed to sparkle in the darkness, but it was probably the moon playing tricks.

With her truck facing the road, Astrid pulled out ahead of

him. He trailed her across the bridge, and then she watched him make a left off the bridge while she turned right. When had pizza and bottled water ever tasted so good?

She bit her lip as she glanced at the time on the dashboard. Olly would probably be sleeping by now, but maybe he'd appreciate that she hadn't called to check on him his first night. She'd call one of the Scout leaders when she got home just to make sure all went well on the first day. They didn't have to tell Olly she called.

Now that the thieves had stolen the drone from Jimmy's Auto, she felt confident that they were the ones who'd launched the drone and not Olly. She had no clue why they hadn't thought about the memory card when they dumped it in her trash. They could've saved themselves a lot of trouble.

She dabbled her fingers against the small lump on the back of her head—and could've saved her some pain.

She veered onto the long drive leading to Tate's cabin and parked behind his Jeep. She climbed out of the truck and locked it. As she stepped toward the porch, she jerked her head toward a rustling noise from the bushes beyond the firepit.

A dog had been nosing around the property for the past few weeks, but Olly had scared him off when he ran after him to see if he had a collar. Maybe the dog had come back. They'd left some food for him, which was gone the following day, but that could've been any wild animal.

As she crept toward the bushes, she called softly. "Come out, baby. I'm not going to hurt you."

She crouched down, and someone slammed her from behind, knocking her to her knees. With his hand splayed across the back of her head, gloved fingers digging into her scalp, he shoved her forward, face in the dirt.

She scooped in a breath to scream and choked on the dirt she inhaled. She twisted her body to throw off her attacker, and that's when she felt it—a sharp point to her neck.

In a raspy voice, her assailant whispered in her ear. "Give me the memory card for that drone, or I'll slit your throat."

Chapter Eight

West reached for his phone on the console, his fingers tapping along the surface, surprised Deputy Fletcher hadn't called him with the update after separating the couple and talking to the victim.

Easing off the gas, West glanced at the console. Then the cup holder. Then the passenger seat. He felt the front pocket of his flannel shirt, and then hit the steering wheel with the heel of his hand. His phone must've fallen out of his pocket in the back of Astrid's truck.

He hadn't heard it ring since he left her, so it wasn't hiding in this vehicle. Knowing two deputies were already at the scene, West made a U-turn. He wouldn't even have to bother Astrid. He'd leave his car running and grab his phone from the truck bed. It had to be there.

In less than five minutes, he passed the bridge and kept going. He turned on his high beams so he wouldn't miss the entrance to her cabin. Not wanting to disturb her, he dialed back on the headlights as he turned onto the drive.

His lights swept over her truck as he pulled up beside it. Leaving his engine idling, he pushed open the door and planted one foot on the ground.

A scream pierced the air, and his body startled to attention. "Astrid?"

A commotion erupted on the other side of the firepit, a thrashing of bushes and someone choking. With his flashlight in the car and the headlights illuminating a different area, he pulled his weapon from its holster. He stalked toward the noise, his eyes straining to see into the dark. "Who's there? Come out."

"West!" Astrid staggered toward him, her hand to her throat. "He went into the woods."

He lowered his gun and rushed toward her, catching her with one arm. He led her toward the driveway into the glare of the headlights. "Are you all right? What happened to your neck?"

Her eyes widened, and she looked like the proverbial deer caught by surprise. "My neck. It's fine. Go get him."

He eyed the bushes where she'd come from, not even stirring now. "I can't chase after someone in the dark… and I'm not leaving you here by yourself. Let's sit on the porch. Tell me what happened."

As he put an arm around her and led her to the house, she leaned into him, her body conforming to his. He settled her on the step and swallowed hard when he spotted another drop of blood creeping down her throat. He touched the dark red bead with the tip of his finger. "What did he do?"

Her gaze darted to the forest. "He held a knife to my throat. He shoved my face into the ground."

Pointing to the cameras above them, he asked, "Do you think your security cameras caught anything?"

She shook her head and sucked in a breath. "He attacked me where you saw me—in the dark. The camera may have recorded the scuffle, but I doubt we'll be able to see anything of substance."

Brushing his knuckles down her cheek to dislodge some dirt, he asked, "What did he want? Did he say anything?"

A sob caught in her throat, and she coughed. "It's the drone again. He wants the memory card."

West's heart skipped a few beats. "He just stole the drone and presumably the memory card with it."

"Presumably."

"Did you have a chance to answer him? Tell him you didn't have it?" A pulse throbbed at the base of his throat.

"I told him I didn't have the card, that it was in the drone the last time I had it." She clasped a hand around her neck. "That's when he pricked me with the point of the knife… and then you drove up."

"Thank God I did. I think I dropped my phone in your truck bed." He drove a knuckle against his jaw. "What the hell is going on with this drone? This isn't some teenage kids trying to avoid incriminating themselves. And what happened to the memory card? It was there when you got the drone from Davia, right?"

"Of course it was." She pressed the heel of her hand to her forehead. "Everything was fine when I checked it out from the office—memory card in the slot, no dents or scratches, in working order. All hell broke loose when someone broke into my house to steal it, changed their mind and dumped it in my trash can. I thought this was over with the theft at Jimmy's."

"This is far from over. Once I get you settled in the house, I'll have a look out there with my flashlight." He tipped his head toward the black expanse of forest. He had zero confidence he'd find anything with the beam of his flashlight, but he couldn't sit here and do nothing after Astrid had been attacked—again.

She grabbed a wooden post and pulled herself to her feet. "I'm not settling anywhere. I'm coming with you. I know the forest better than you."

"Just stick with me." He didn't want to let this woman out of his sight.

"Wait. What happened to the call?" She ran her fingers through her hair, dislodging dirt and bits of debris from the ground.

"It was a domestic. A couple of my deputies were handling it. I'm sure they're doing fine." He jerked his thumb over his shoulder. "If my phone is, in fact, in the back of your truck, I'll give them a call."

As she brushed off her clothes, he turned off his idling SUV and grabbed his flashlight. He used it to scan the bed of Astrid's truck, and the light caught his phone's screen. "It's here. Must've been fate or something that made me forget it."

When she didn't answer, he spun around, his heart thumping. When her front door opened, he nearly sagged against the bumper of the truck in relief.

"Did you find your phone?" She jogged down the front steps, stuffing her arms into another jacket, a flashlight of her own clutched in one hand.

"Yeah, it was there." He held up one finger. "Hang on."

While making his call to Fletch, he kept his eyes on Astrid as she approached the tree line of the forest. West explained the situation and verified that the deputies had the domestic in hand. Then he pocketed his phone and joined Astrid.

"All set on that other call." He aimed his light at the ground. "Did it start here? Did you see where he came from?"

"I came over here to investigate a noise. He approached me from behind, so I couldn't see him. He had gloves on, and his voice sounded muffled so I'm guessing he was wearing the balaclava again."

"You think it's the same guy from last night?" He crouched down, examining the signs of a struggle—disturbed dirt, broken twigs, a drop of blood.

"I hope so. I'd hate to think there's more than one guy after me." As she rose to her feet she listed to the side, and West caught her around the waist.

"You sure you're up to this? I can handle a quick look by myself." He dropped his hand from her hip and took a step back, aware that everything about her was drawing him in closer. "Or are you worried about being in the house by yourself?"

She hooked her thumbs in her front pocket. "I'm okay in the house. The security system is good, and there are several guns in there—which I know how to use."

"I don't doubt it." He gestured with his flashlight. "If you want to lead the way, I'll be right behind you."

"If he came through the forest, which I think he did, he would've come this way. There's a path that we use." She held a branch to the side for him, and he stepped after her.

"What noise got your attention? I'd think after last night's attack, you might've been a little more careful."

She stopped suddenly, and he plowed into her back. "Sorry."

Twisting her head over her shoulder, she said, "I honestly thought my stalker was done with me after he got the drone from Jimmy's. I was almost happy he stole the damned thing. How was I supposed to know he wanted more?"

"Yeah, I get it." He held up his hands. "But what was the noise that lured you out?"

"Rustling in the bushes. I thought it was a dog that's been hanging around here recently. Olly scared him off last time, just when I thought he'd come to us. He looks a little ragged, and I was hoping to lure him in to feed him and maybe get him checked out by a vet, see if he's chipped." She shrugged.

"Instead, you're the one who got lured. Did you tell anyone about the dog?"

Her head snapped up. "No. I mean, I don't know. I guess so. You think the person who held a knife to my throat knew I'd come out for the dog?"

"He *was* able to get you away from the house and the cameras."

Looking at the ground and scanning it with his light, West followed Astrid as she moved forward.

She snorted. "I think that was just luck on his part. What he probably figured was that I'd been lured into a false sense of security because I no longer had the drone—and he was spot-on. I just can't figure out why this person is interested in that footage."

"Too bad the video wasn't uploaded to a computer or phone. Then we'd be able to find out. You need to ask your coworkers about what they captured on the drone." His pulse jumped and he tugged on the waistband of Astrid's jeans to stop her. "Hold on. Watch your step."

She paused with her foot raised, wobbling on one leg. "Literally, don't take another step?"

"My flashlight picked up something shiny right by your left foot. Do you see it?" He flickered the beam of his light at the ground and saw the gleam of something silver in the dirt. "There it is."

Astrid hopped out of the way, and West squatted, pulling on a glove he'd taken from his car. He sifted his gloved fingers through the leaves and pebbles until they stumbled on a rectangular shape. He rescued it, bobbling a lighter in his palm. "It's a lighter. Looks new and shiny."

Astrid crouched beside him, her knee banging against his thigh. "I recognize that."

"This belongs to you or someone you know?"

"We probably have one in the house. Turn it over. It's from the Salty Crab."

West nudged the lighter over in his palm. Yellow print stamped on the blue background proclaimed the lighter as property of the Salty Crab. "It looks new, not like it's been sitting out here for months or even weeks."

"You think it could belong to my assailant? I was getting ready to read Olly the riot act for stealing the lighter from the house and bringing it out here." She huffed out a breath, and the hair hanging over her shoulder stirred.

"We'd better check your house for the lighter first. Let's turn back." He dug a baggie from the pocket of his shirt and dropped the lighter inside. "I can check this for prints if you're not missing your lighter."

She started to rise, and then grabbed his arm, her fingers digging into his shirt. "Did you hear that noise?"

His muscles coiled as he cocked his head. Some leaves crackled and a twig snapped. As he moved his hand over his holstered weapon, the intruder whined and panted. He dropped his hand. "That's either your stray dog, or there's a wolf out here."

"We don't have wolves on the island. The population was eradicated years ago, and they haven't returned." She hunched forward. "Here, boy. C'mon out. I'll feed you."

The whining stopped, and a raggedy shepherd mix emerged from a clump of bushes.

Astrid whispered. "There you are. You want food?"

"Maybe he'll follow us. Too bad I don't have any of the pepperoni on me." West rose slowly. "Let's start walking."

As they turned, the dog stiffened his posture, and his eyes gleamed in the dark. With its pointy ears and sharp muzzle, this guy could pass as a wolf.

They crept back toward the house, and the dog followed them warily, ready to bolt at the slightest provocation.

When they reached the driveway, Astrid held her finger to her lips. "I'll go inside and get some food. I have leftover chicken."

"I'm not sure he'll be happy with my company alone. I'll come with you. Then you can direct me to your security footage, so that I can check the attack."

They both walked into the house with the dog frozen just steps from the porch. Astrid peeled off toward the kitchen and jabbed her finger at her laptop on the counter. "I'll get you logged on after I grab some chicken for my new best friend."

He sat at the counter in front of the computer as she ducked into the fridge. She emerged with a plastic bag in her hand, and then leaned over his shoulder.

She entered her password and clicked on a logo in the lower-left corner of the desktop. "You can look through the footage here from tonight."

He called after her. "Leave the front door wide open, and don't go running after that mutt into the woods if he takes off."

"How dare you call him a mutt." She clicked her tongue, but she left her door open.

As he started to scroll through the security cam footage, West could hear her murmuring to the beast. If that dog had an ounce of sense, he'd follow that woman anywhere.

After several seconds, the dog's nails clicked on the hardwood floor of the cabin, and Astrid shut the door. "Got him inside. He's ravenous. Probably thirsty, too."

"At least someone got lucky tonight." West pushed the laptop away from him, stood up and stretched.

At her wide-eyed gaze and pink cheeks, he clarified. "I did not get lucky with that recording. If you're looking, and I was, you can see sort of a scuffle of movement and maybe even a figure, but I can't make out a thing beyond that. He knew about the security camera."

"Yeah, because he avoided it the other day when he broke the window on the side door." Astrid knelt next to a bowl, the dog sniffing her heels, and shredded the rest of the chicken into it. She filled another bowl with water and placed it next to the food.

Whatever reservations the dog had earlier evaporated. Maybe he witnessed the attack on Astrid. He gobbled the food and took a few laps of water.

"You plan on keeping him here, right?" West eyed the beast and his sharp teeth.

"I do. I'm going to take him to the vet tomorrow, see if he's chipped. If he belongs to someone, I want to return him to his family." She wedged a hand on her hip. "Why? You called him a mutt before."

"He is a mutt, but he's a mutt who might just have your back out here by yourself."

She rolled her eyes. "I'm safe inside."

"You're not safe outside—at night. I'll feel a little better if the pooch is here with you. He looks like he can hold his own."

"Why, thank you, Sheriff."

He didn't miss her Southern twang...or her irony. "And if you do have a gun here, maybe you should load it and keep it with you. With Olly out of the house, that should be safe."

"Olly knows how to use a gun and knows all about gun safety. He knows better than to touch a gun—loaded or otherwise."

A sharp pain lanced West's temple, and he jabbed two fingers against it to massage it away. "You should always be careful."

Narrowing her eyes at him, she said, "Of course."

"I'm going to take this to the station with me." He dangled the baggie in the air before shoving it back into his pocket. "Maybe we can get some prints from this guy. We're still going to process Jimmy's garage."

"Lock your doors, arm yourself and you—" West crouched before the dog and chucked it under the chin "—earn your keep around here and act like a watchdog."

"I'll give him some more food, so he knows where his loyalty lies." Astrid took a tentative step toward the door.

How did you end an evening that was not quite a date and had turned into another rescue mission? He could see himself out and didn't expect a kiss or even a hug—didn't mean he didn't want one, or both. Astrid's phone buzzed on the counter, saving them both an awkward farewell.

She gave it a cursory glance, and then did a double take. "It's one of the Scout leaders."

Her panicked tone gave him pause, and he planted his feet on the floor. She didn't need any more stress tonight.

"Porter? What's wrong? Is Olly okay?"

West watched as her face regained some of its earlier color, and her chest heaved. "Okay, okay. That's fine. Do you think he's scared or homesick?"

She chewed on a nail as she listened. "Yeah, put him on. I'll wait."

He raised his eyebrows. "Everything okay?"

"Porter, one of the Scout leaders, just called to tell me Olly requested a phone call with me." She tapped the display to put the phone on speaker and refilled the dog's dish with more chicken.

Olly's high-low voice squawked out of the speaker, filling the kitchen. "Mom?"

"How's it going, kiddo? Miss me?" Astrid kept her tone light, but the crease between her eyebrows told a different story.

"Mom, I have to tell you something. I wanted to tell you before, but, umm, I thought maybe you wouldn't let me go on the camping trip."

Astrid's blue eyes flashed, but West couldn't tell if they signaled anger or fear.

"Go on. I'm sure it's not as bad as you think. Nothing we can't figure out together and deal with when you get home. Spill it, kiddo."

West marveled at her vocal control as the emotions played out over her face.

Olly continued, dragging out his words. "You know the drone?"

Astrid's body stiffened, and she picked up the phone. "Yes, I know the drone."

"I took it, Mom."

Astrid shot West a quick glance and swallowed. "When did you take it?"

"Logan and I rode our bikes back to the house. I had my key, so I let myself in."

"Wait, wait, wait." Astrid waved her hand in the air, and the dog perked up his ears. "How'd you get past the camera? It didn't pick you up."

"Ah, I didn't set the security system when we left earlier, so I just got in with the key. We took the drone and rode our bikes to the cliff over Crystal Cove. Then we flew the drone." He ended on a hiccup.

"Olly." Astrid sank to a stool at the kitchen island. "You broke it? How'd it get in the trash can at home?"

"Didn't have time to put it away when we got back, so I put it in the trash. I-I didn't break that window, though. I don't know how that happened, Mom. I swear. I didn't know someone would break in the house and that you'd be looking for the drone right away. So I sneaked outside to get it."

"But you broke it, Olly."

"I didn't really break it, Mom. It wasn't us."

"Don't make things worse by lying to me Olly. I know the drone is broken. I tried to use it today."

"I know, Mom, but we didn't break it. That man broke it."

Astrid put her hand flat against her chest as West moved closer to the phone. "What man, Olly?"

"That man on the beach at Crystal Cove—the same day that body was found."

Chapter Nine

A seed of dread formed in Astrid's gut, and one look at West's face told her he had the same feeling. She couldn't quite pinpoint her fear yet, but Olly's confession had sent a ripple of it down her back.

She peeled her tongue off the roof of her mouth. "What man, Olly?"

"Just some guy on the beach. I flew the drone off the cliff and it kinda dipped down, and we couldn't see it anymore. I thought maybe it went into the water. Me and Logan didn't want to get too close to the edge, but we moved to where we could see the rocks. I heard someone yelling, and I think he hit the drone with something. By the time I got it back up, it was flying funny. Then I landed it and saw the dent in the side. I'm sorry, Mom. I'll pay for it and everything out of my own money."

West cleared his throat. "Olly, this is Sheriff Chandler. Can you tell me what time you were on the cliff with the drone?"

Olly hiccupped again, and Astrid figured her son was freaking out about the sheriff on the line.

"Wh-what? Am I gonna get arrested for flying the drone?"

"Not at all, Olly." West massaged his temples. "Can you remember what time you were there?"

Olly released a noisy breath. "Naw. It was after my mom dropped me at Logan's house and before we rode back to his house so his mom could take us to the Spring Fling."

West mouthed some words at her that looked as if he were asking her if she could figure out the approximate time. She could, and she nodded.

"That's okay. That's good enough. One more question for you, Olly." West closed his eyes. "Did you see the man who yelled at you or what he was doing on the beach?"

Olly paused so long, Astrid thought he'd hung up. She said, "Olly?"

"Yeah, um, no. I really didn't see him. Maybe the top of his head. He was wearing a black beanie though, so I didn't see his hair. We didn't see anything else."

West pinched the bridge of his nose. "Did he see you?"

"N-no. We ducked down 'cuz he was yelling something at us, but we couldn't understand what he was saying."

Rubbing her aching jaw, Astrid asked, "And that's when you went home? You went right home after that and dumped the drone in the garbage can?"

"Yeah. Sorry, Mom. I felt bad, so I wanted to tell you. But we didn't break the window, and it wasn't broken when we were there." Olly yawned loudly.

"Okay, well, don't worry about it now. Have fun at camp, and we'll figure out how you're going to repay Davia for the drone. Got it?"

"Yeah, yeah. G'night. Bye, Sheriff."

Porter got back on the phone and assured Astrid that he'd see Olly back to his tent.

When Astrid ended the call, she placed the phone back

on the counter and stared at it. Without looking at West, she asked, "What are you thinking?"

He didn't answer right away, and her throat closed. She peeked at him from beneath her eyelashes. "Just say it. It can't be any worse than what I'm already thinking."

"Olly and Logan may have stumbled upon Chase's murder without knowing it. The killer saw the drone and struck out at it, hoping to bring it down, hoping the drone video wasn't going to someone's phone. He didn't mention hearing any popping sounds though, so he couldn't have heard the actual murder."

She clutched her neck with one hand. "When he couldn't knock down the drone, he followed them or somehow figured out where Olly lived and has been trying to get the drone back ever since."

"Thought he hit pay dirt in Jimmy's garage only to discover the video card wasn't in the drone."

"Where is it?" Astrid crossed her arms and dug her fingernails into her biceps. "That card was in the drone when I took it from the office. I checked."

"Maybe when the guy smashed the drone, the card fell out. We know he whacked the sleeve where you insert the card. It might be on that beach…or in the water."

She lifted her shoulders to her ears. "How do we tell *him* that? How far is he willing to go to find it? He broke into my house, attacked me at my truck, stole the drone from Jimmy's and went at me again in my own driveway."

"The good news is, if we find that card, we've solved Chase's murder."

"If we find it before he does." She rubbed her arms, feeling cold ever since Olly's call. "What if he thinks Olly and Logan got a good look at him?"

"He must know by now they didn't. They weren't the ones who reported Chase's body on the beach. The killer has to figure that two boys would call in a dead body." He cocked his head, his hazel eyes probing her face. "Why? Do you think Olly is lying about not seeing the man?"

She pinched her chin as she watched the dog dip his head for more water. "I don't think he was lying about that, but he seemed a little off to me—like maybe he wasn't telling me the whole truth and nothin' but."

"Kids lie all the time." West dashed a hand through his hair. "I-I mean, sometimes they lie about stupid stuff."

Astrid widened her eyes. "Do you have children?"

"Uh, no." He raised one hand. "But I was one."

"Well, I hope it's something minor like he ate too many s'mores tonight and got a stomachache and not that he witnessed a murder on the beach." She aimed a toe at the dog, collapsed at her feet. "What do you think? Should I let him stay inside tonight?"

"He looks like the type of dog that's not going to let anything get past him. Keep him inside…for security. And where's that weapon you were talking about before? One of your brother's guns in the safe?"

"Oh, no. I have my own. It's under my bed right now. When Tate, my brother, is home, I leave it in his safe, but when I'm here by myself I like to keep it handy." Astrid swallowed. She didn't want to reveal too much to West about her previous life with her ex stalking her. It would probably make him turn and run the other way, which maybe he should do, anyway.

"Arm your security system when I leave and keep your dog and your gun close." He crouched down and rubbed the dog's neck, prompting him to thump his tail on the kitchen floor without opening his eyes. "What are you going to name him?"

"I don't want to name him anything until I make sure he doesn't already have a home and a family looking for him. I haven't seen any lost-dog posters, though, and he's been hanging around here for a few weeks."

"Too bad he wasn't hanging around when your intruder dropped by."

"I hadn't fed him yet. Now he's going to have some fur in the game." She knelt beside West and scratched the dog behind his ear. "Are you going to look for the video card on the beach?"

"Might as well give it a try. Should probably check the bluff where Olly launched the drone, too. It could be anywhere." West pushed to his feet and wiped his hands on the thighs of his jeans. "I need to wash my hands. If I touch my face after touching dog, I'm gonna have itchy eyes."

"Help yourself." She waved her hand at the kitchen sink. "Do you have any leads in the Chase Thompson case? Any…witnesses, besides that drone, prints, weapons, clues?"

"A few things have come up." He squirted some lemon hand soap into his palm and lathered his hands under a stream of water. "I think the motive is most likely drugs. Chase was a small-time dealer. Almost everyone knows that. The question is if he graduated to the big leagues and got in over his head."

"So this person who's after me is most likely not a local, or at least not a Dead Falls resident. He may be local to Discovery Bay." She gave the dog a final pat before standing up next to West as he ripped a paper towel from the roll to dry his hands. "You'll keep me posted, won't you? I mean, about the memory card."

"I will keep you posted." He balled up the paper towel and held it up. She pointed to the drawer that pulled out for the kitchen trash can. After he tossed it, he brushed his hands together. "You going to be okay here tonight on your own?"

"As you mentioned—" she aimed a finger at the dog, lounging at her feet "—I'm not going to be on my own."

"You should come into the station tomorrow for another report about tonight's events. Might as well have a legal trail of all these incidents. Just in case."

"In case he kills me one of these times?" She'd tried to keep her voice light but she'd failed, and a rash of goose bumps pimpled her arms.

"Don't even joke about that, Astrid. I...we'll keep you safe." He chucked the dog under the chin and made a move toward the front door.

She followed West, and the dog's nails clicked on the hardwood floor as he trailed after both of them. Looked like the mangy mutt already didn't want to let her out of his sight.

She stepped out on the porch with him. "Thanks for the pizza and for coming back here—even if it was for your phone."

"And thanks for showing me the place at Misty Hollow. Not sure it's for me, but when I see something I like I'll let you know so you can rep me."

"You haven't seen anything you liked so far?"

"Oh, I wouldn't say that." He clumped down the steps of the porch and strode to his SUV.

With her heart beating faster than usual, she watched

him get into his vehicle and lift a hand in a wave. She waved back and slipped into the house. After setting the security system, she leaned against the door and eyed the dog, who thumped his tail once.

"Do you think he meant me, boy?"

THE FOLLOWING MORNING, Astrid awakened to a whine close to her ear. She jerked back, pulling her pillow in front of her as an inadequate shield. One glimpse of the wet nose at the edge of the bed, and memories of last night flooded over her.

She traced the small scratch on her throat with her fingertip. What would've happened if West hadn't forgotten his phone? The sheriff always seemed to be in the right place at the right time—for her.

At a second, more insistent cry, Astrid rolled out of bed and patted the dog's head, his fur rough and wiry beneath her fingers. "I hope you're house-trained and didn't have any accidents last night. Of course, that would totally be my fault."

He trotted after her as she went downstairs. She slid open the back door, and the dog dashed outside. He made a beeline for the woods and disappeared.

She sighed, leaving the sliding door open behind her. Maybe he was destined to be a wild dog. She'd try to lure him back later with more food, but she made a note to pick up a leash and collar so she could take him to the vet—if he'd let her.

At least there had been no more incidents last night. She twisted her head over her shoulder, taking in the wide-open door, and pivoted to close and lock it. The dog would be able to find his way back to the house if he wanted. He'd been sniffing around for weeks.

As she stuck a bowl of oatmeal in the microwave, her cell phone rang. Her shoulders tensed when she saw the unknown number. "Hello, this is Astrid."

"Astrid, this is Michelle Clark. I'm calling about the Misty Hollow property you have listed for sale."

Astrid opened and closed her mouth like a fish, grateful the client couldn't see her. They hadn't even posted aerial pictures of the property yet. Maybe she wouldn't need those drone pics after all. "Um, yes, of course. Would you like to see it? I have to warn you. It's a fixer. The owner didn't want to make any improvements before listing, but the asking price reflects that."

She clamped down on her lower lip. She was supposed to be talking up the property, not leading with all the bad.

"Understood, and I *would* like to see it. Are you available today? I'm on Dead Falls Island just for a few days and would love to have a look before I leave."

Astrid pulled back her shoulders. Time to get serious. "And I would love to show it to you. I'm available this afternoon. I can pick you up at your hotel—or wherever you're staying."

"That would be perfect. Let's make it three o'clock, and you can pick me up at the Bay View Hotel. Is that convenient for you?"

"I'll swing by there at three. Please call me if anything changes. Otherwise, I'll see you then, Michelle."

Astrid ended the call, clapped her hands and twirled around the kitchen. She'd make it up to Davia by selling this property in record time.

She spent the morning at the sheriff's station to make

a report about the attack last night. She'd craned her neck around the small station, but West was nowhere to be found.

She also stopped by the pet store and bought a collar and leash to corral her stray. While in the shop she perused the lost animals board, but nobody had posted missing a brown-and-black shepherd mix.

Her final stop before picking up her client was the office. She'd already called Davia that morning with the bad news about the stolen drone, but her boss hadn't seemed concerned at all. She had her eyes on a new toy, one that would send the video straight to a phone or computer.

Astrid sailed into the office and gave Davia a thumbs-up. "I'm showing the Misty Hollow property in about thirty minutes."

Sumit kicked his legs up on his desk, crossing them at the ankles. "Since you broke our drone, you'd better make good."

Astrid made a face at him. "You're just jealous because Shannon picked me."

"That dump?" Sumit snorted. "You can have it, sister, and good luck."

"Michelle Clark called here, asking for you. I gave her your number." Davia held up her hands, fingers crossed. "Let's hope she's serious, unlike the sheriff."

"How'd you know the sheriff wasn't serious?" Astrid flicked through some files on her desk just in case Michelle wanted to make an offer on the spot.

"Mmm, I just got the impression he wanted to spend a little more time with you." Davia winked broadly.

Astrid dropped a folder. "Are you kidding?"

"No. Are you clueless? Didn't you two go out to dinner?"

"If you call pizza at Luigi's out to dinner, and we were interrupted by Jimmy, anyway."

"That's a date in my book." Sumit crossed his hands behind his head. "In fact, that's a high-end date in my book."

"I didn't realize you ever got past coffee date one with any of your online honeys. Maybe you should start with Luigi's, and you'd make some progress."

"Did the new sheriff make progress with you?" Sumit formed pistols with both hands and pointed at her.

"That's enough, children." Davia pointed to the whiteboard. "Astrid, don't forget to put your details on the board."

"Of course." Anxious to get off the topic of her and West, Astrid walked to the whiteboard and uncapped a marker, the alcohol smell invading her nose. She wrote down the address of the property, the time of the showing, Michelle's name and phone number. The agents in the office never showed a property without notifying everyone else on this board...except last night. Sheriffs could be the exception, although Astrid knew more than most that a uniform didn't exempt the wearer from bad deeds.

"Maybe we won't even have to list this one." Davia held up a finger and answered her cell.

As Davia sweet-talked a client and Sumit grabbed his own call, Astrid slid all her files into her bag and waved to them on her way out of the office. Before she started the engine of Tate's Jeep, she texted Michelle that she was on her way.

Traffic on the main road crawled with tourists and outdoor enthusiasts, hitting the island for spring break. The hotels, restaurants, bars, bait shops and tour guides loved it, but the rest of the locals grinned with gritted teeth. The tourists were a necessary evil, but they did buy summer cabins on the island. Of course, if the big development company Bradford and Son had its way, they'd be looking at even more traffic.

She turned into the parking lot of the Bay View Hotel and spotted Michelle in front immediately, black hair pinned into a chic chignon at the nape of her neck and oversize black sunglasses tempering the glare of the overcast day.

Astrid glided up to the curb and rolled down the window. "Michelle? I'm Astrid Mitchell."

"Oh, you're good." She grabbed the handle of the passenger door. "How'd you know it was me?"

Astrid caught a whiff of Michelle's exotic perfume as she slid onto the leather seat. "You didn't look like you were waiting for a fishing or camping tour."

"Ah, yes. City girl." Michelle waved a hand over her black slacks and white blouse. Tapping her high heel, she asked, "I suppose these are unpractical for touring the property, aren't they?"

"There are a lot of unpaved areas of the property." Astrid wrinkled her nose. "I'd hate for you to ruin those beautiful shoes."

"Give me one moment?" Michelle held up one perfectly peach-colored manicured finger. "I'll run back inside and make a few adjustments."

"Take your time."

As she watched Michelle stride purposefully back to the hotel entrance, not one single wobble on those heels, Astrid tried to place the woman's accent. It was as exotic as her heavy perfume that still hung in the car.

A text notification came through on her phone, and she bit the inside of her cheek as she read West's message. He hadn't had any luck locating the drone's memory card on the beach or the bluff.

She texted him back that she'd have a look in and around her trash can on the side of the house. If Olly had stuffed the drone back in its box out there, maybe the card fell out.

By the time she put her phone down, Michelle was making a beeline for the Jeep, a pair of dark jeans encasing her long legs and a pair of low-heeled boots replacing the heels. She hadn't changed her white blouse or jacket, so she still looked elegant.

Michelle pulled open the door. "Better?"

"I think you'll be much more comfortable." Astrid plugged her dying phone into the car's charger and pulled back onto the road, apologizing for the traffic. "It's not much better in the summer, but the visitors are more spread out. Are you looking for a permanent residence or a vacation spot?"

"Vacation spot. My husband recently discovered boating and with that fishing." She rolled her dark eyes. "I told him the only condition was that I had to find or at least approve of the place."

"That sounds like a good deal."

Michelle's large, square-cut diamond glittered as she fluttered her hands around the car. "We make our compromises. Are you married?"

Astrid licked her dry lips. "Divorced."

Michelle clicked her tongue. "Ditto for me. Twice before Charles. So, we know, marriage is all about compromise."

Marriage was also about your husband not being a criminal and a thief. Astrid allowed a smile to curve her lips as she nodded.

It sounded like Michelle and her husband had money,

and that's all that mattered to this sale. The more money, the better. She couldn't have a penny-pinching client who would balk at the level of renovations needed to make this property habitable—and to erase its ghoulish past.

They chatted easily on the ride, and Michelle gasped as they approached Dead Falls. Her big diamond glistened like a drop of water from the falls as she put a hand to her mouth. "Can you stop on the bridge for a second so we can admire the view?"

"I can't stop on the bridge, but there's a lookout point to the right once we cross."

With no cars behind them, Astrid crawled across the bridge so Michelle could gawk. Once across, she turned right and backed into the turnout where she and West had parked last night. If he hadn't gotten that call, would the night have taken a romantic turn?

Michelle rolled down her window and stuck her head out. "This is lovely. I suppose there's no view of this from the property, is there?"

"I'm afraid not. It's not on an incline, but the good news is that you don't get as much moisture there as you do in this area."

"You're right." Michelle drew her head back inside the car and patted her hair. "This could give major frizz."

Astrid slid a glance at Michelle's perfect coif as she pulled back onto the road. "Just another five minutes."

She drove onto the property with less trepidation than last night. The structures didn't look as spooky during the day, but she'd have to tell Michelle the whole sordid story.

She pulled up and parked in the same spot as last night with a view of the main house and the charred barn, the other buildings visible in the rear. As she put a hand on

Michelle's arm, she said, "We need to discuss something before I show you the property and you potentially fall in love with it."

"Oh, sweetie—" Michelle flicked her long fingernails as an accent Astrid still couldn't place in person touched her words "—I know all about the storied history of this place. My husband, Charles, and I compromise, but he would never allow me to check out a place without doing his research. So, yes, I'm aware of the family massacre that took place here many years ago, and that the perpetrator, who'd gotten away with it, remained on this island and started killing single mothers in some sort of weird retribution."

"Whew." Astrid skimmed her fingertips across her forehead. "I'm glad to get that out of the way. I'm not looking forward to that part of this sale."

Michelle scooted her dark glasses to the edge of her nose. "Weren't you scared?"

"Me?" Astrid pressed her hand against her chest. "Why would I be scared?"

"He was going after single mothers, wasn't he?" She arched a perfect dark eyebrow.

Astrid jerked her head back. She'd told Michelle she was divorced but hadn't mentioned Olly. "How do you know I'm a single mom?"

Michelle pulled down the visor and tapped the picture of Olly wedged under the mirror. "I saw this earlier. He looks just like you."

"Oh." Astrid cracked a smile. "That's Olly. He's ten."

"Cute boy." Michelle readjusted her sunglasses. "So, weren't you afraid when Brian Lamar started killing single moms?"

"Not really." Astrid put her hand on the door handle and pulled it, cracking open the door. "The two women he murdered were involved with drugs, so a lot of us figured that was the link."

"So sad." Michelle shook her head. "I have a son who's an addict. No fun."

"I'm sorry to hear that." Astrid pushed open the door. "Now that the bad stuff is out of the way, let's focus on the good. Shall we?"

Their shoes crunched the gravel and dirt as they approached the main house. It didn't take long to show Michelle the house, as she'd already admitted they'd be tearing it down and rebuilding a new structure.

Michelle took a longer time surveying the aspect of the rest of the property and the outbuildings—its positioning, its views, the property line. The history didn't seem to faze her at all.

She had been snapping several photos with her phone and raised it for another shot. She cursed and dropped the phone in her bag. "I knew it was going to die on me. Charles will kill me if I don't get pictures of everything. Can I borrow your phone for a sec or tell you what pics I want?"

Patting her purse, Astrid said, "Mine was dying, too. I left it in the car on the charger, even though it's not charging now."

"I'll run and get it, sweetie." Michelle called over her shoulder. "Jeep unlocked?"

"It is, yes."

While Michelle returned to the car to get Astrid's phone, Astrid inspected the burned-out barn, the wood still giving off an acrid odor. She'd have to talk to Shannon again about knocking this down. It created an eyesore for anyone immediately coming onto the property.

Astrid jumped when Michelle came up behind her.

"Lost in thought?" Michelle handed Astrid's phone to her.

"Just thinking how I'm going to convince the seller to tear this down. If she doesn't mind, I might just hire my own crew of locals to do the job and write it off as the cost of doing business." Astrid navigated to her camera with her thumb. "What do you need?"

At Michelle's direction, Astrid took several photos of the property and texted them all to Michelle's number.

"Thank you so much." Michelle plucked the phone from her purse, seemed to remember it was dead and dropped it back inside. "Those should satisfy Charles."

"If he'd like to have a look himself, I'd be happy to make myself available."

Michelle answered, "Let's see what he thinks, first."

As they walked toward the car together, Michelle said, "It's certainly big enough for what we want. The views, even though we can't see the falls, are fantastic. There's so much we could do with this."

"I agree. It hasn't been utilized to its full potential. It's just waiting for the right owners to come along and—" Astrid snapped her fingers "—reimagine it."

"I like that notion." Michelle tripped to a stop, her head bending forward. "Oh!"

"Are you all right?" Astrid put a hand on Michelle's back.

"Did you drop this, sweetie?" Michelle crouched down and rose with her hand cupped.

Astrid peered into her palm and sucked in a quick breath. "I-it's a memory card."

Chapter Ten

A smear of blood from Naomi Wakefield's ragged finger-nail, with its chipped blue polish, marred the sleeve of her hoodie as she folded her arms tightly against her chest.

West dragged his gaze away from the red spot and focused on Naomi's face, black smudges beneath her eyes, the tip of her nose a cherry red.

He cleared his throat. "When was the last time you saw Chase, Naomi?"

"That morning before he…died." She glanced over her bony shoulder into the forest. "You're not gonna tell anyone I talked to you, are you?"

"I already told you. There's no reason for me to go public, but if you provide some material evidence that can help convict someone, you'll need to testify in court. But let's not go there right now. I'm just trying to establish a timeline for Chase, and you seem to be the last person who saw him alive."

"Other than the guy who killed him." Her bloody thumb went back to her lips, and she bared her teeth to tug at her cuticle.

"What time did he leave your place?" As he waited for her answer, he took inventory of the sad woman before him—her pasty complexion, her jiggling leg, the random twitch of her left eye. Could the murder of her boyfriend prompt her to go to rehab for her meth addiction? Was that rock bottom enough for her?

Tucking a lock of stringy blond hair behind one ear, she said, "Maybe eleven o'clock, like in the morning. I just got up."

"Did he tell you where he was going or who he was meeting?" He nudged the can of Coke he'd brought for her just to get her to stop gnawing at her own flesh.

"No, but it was big. He was excited. I don't think this was the first time, though. He got his hands on some primo stuff a few weeks before. He'd been selling it around the island, even gave me a little taste of it." She spread her thin lips into a smile that stretched across her narrow face and revealed teeth too yellow for a woman her age.

Looked like he'd given Naomi more than a taste. "So, you think he was getting more of this product from someone?"

She hunched her shoulders and squeezed the can, denting one side. "Maybe. He didn't tell me nothing."

"Did you ever see Chase with another phone?" Chase's phone had been missing, but they were working with his carrier on getting the call record for it.

"He was always on the phone. He coulda had two. I accused him of using a burner to call his side chick." Her dull brown eyes flashed for a second. "Did you find his phone?"

"He didn't have it on him." Chase Thompson had more than one woman on call? West scratched his chin. "Did Chase have another girlfriend?"

"Seemed like it to me, but he said he didn't. He was a liar." She slammed the Coke can on the picnic table.

If Chase was seeing another woman, maybe West could

get her name out of Naomi. He coughed. "Could he have left his phone at your place?"

"Not that I know of. I could call it when I get home and listen for it ringing." She rubbed her hands against her thighs. "Can I go now?"

"You can go." He slipped her his card. "If you remember anything, give me a call. We can meet out here again if you like."

"Okay." She stuffed the card in the back pocket of her skinny jeans. "Can you wait here for a bit while I hike back to my car? I don't want anyone seeing you follow me out."

"Go ahead." He fished his phone from his pocket, which had been buzzing with texts. "Keep an eye out for Chase's phone, Naomi, and if you can think of the name of his other girlfriend, let me know."

"All right." She swiped the can from the table and hit the path through the forest back to her car.

West blew out a breath. That woman needed help. Maybe with Chase out of her life, she'd seek it.

He glanced at his phone, and his pulse jumped when he saw some text messages from Astrid from just a few minutes ago. He knew she'd been into the station to file a report about the incident last night, but he didn't know what she'd been up to the rest of the day—not that he had a right to know.

He tapped his phone to call her, and she answered before the first ring finished.

"West, do you have a minute? I'm not interrupting you, am I?"

Her breathy voice jacked up his senses. If she'd been attacked again, he'd have to put 24/7 security on her. "Just finished with something. What's up?"

"I found a memory card."

His protective instincts settled down, but his interest piqued. "*The* memory card?"

"That's just it. I don't know if it's the one from the drone, but what are the odds I randomly find a memory card on the ground?"

"That's what happened?" He pushed up from the picnic bench and paced toward the trail. "Where was it?"

"It was out at the Misty Hollow property. Isn't that weird? You and I were just there last night. We didn't see anything then, but of course, it was pitch black out there."

"Does it look like it could be from the drone?"

"I guess so. It's a standard memory card."

"Wait. Where are you? You haven't looked at it, yet?" He glanced back at the picnic table to make sure he hadn't left anything there, and then plowed onto the trail. He'd given Naomi enough time to get out of here.

"No. I'm sitting in the parking lot of the Bay View Hotel in town. Just dropped off my client. I was showing her around the property when she saw the memory card on the ground."

"The drone wasn't anywhere near there, was it? Misty Hollow isn't very close to where Olly was flying it over Crystal Cove and the cliffs above it."

"Doesn't mean Olly and Logan couldn't have ridden their bikes out that way." She huffed out a breath. "If I find out he went over the bridge and was in Misty Hollow, he's in big trouble—bigger trouble."

West broke through the short trail to the road, where his SUV sat solo. He hadn't expected to see Naomi's car even if he hadn't given her enough time to leave first. She'd been so nervous she'd parked on a different stretch of road and hiked in farther than he did.

"I'm coming over to your place. Do you have an adapter on your computer to read the card?"

"I'm sure I can find one. Tate has a lot of that sort of stuff around. If not, I can take it to the office. We've been transferring the drone images to our computers there with an adapter."

Sliding behind the wheel of his vehicle, West said, "I'm on my way. If you get there first and you can't find an adapter, let me know and I'll swing around to your office instead."

"Okay, I'll meet you there."

On the drive to Astrid's place, West got on his speakerphone with the station to take care of the day's business. Finding and arresting Chase Thompson's killer topped his list of priorities, but Astrid's stalker came in at a close second. He couldn't shake the feeling that his two most pressing matters were related.

He pulled up to the cabin and parked to the side, behind her truck. She must've taken her brother's Jeep to show the property, and he'd gotten here first. He'd use his time to check the woods where her attacker had disappeared last night.

He'd sent a deputy out today to have a look, but he hadn't found anything out of the ordinary, nothing indicating someone had made a quick escape through the trees. No prints on the lighter.

He slammed his car door and made his way to the tree line, looking at the ground on his way. Just like last night, he saw the area where Astrid had scuffled with the intruder—along with shoe prints from the deputy.

He ducked into the woods, his head on a swivel as he eyed the bushes and branches for any ripped clothing or threads. How had the guy made his getaway? Had he parked a vehicle somewhere in a clearing? He didn't have a handle on the layout of the forested area yet, but most of it was connected. He could've crashed through the trees from where he'd met Naomi and probably wound up here.

The path beneath his feet led deeper into the woods with a cut-through to the road. Astrid's attacker must've gone that way, back to…wherever. He couldn't have continued through the forest, unless he was some kind of mountain man living off the land.

West froze at the sound of heavy breathing filtering through the leaves. A whine came from the same direction, and West's tense muscles relaxed when he realized the heavy breathing was actually panting.

He gave a low whistle. "Is that you, boy? Did you get away again?"

The dog wasn't about to show himself to West, and he made a quick and stealthy retreat.

The sound of a car engine had him giving up the search and turning back toward the house to meet Astrid. When he stepped out of the forest, he almost ran into her.

She yelped and smacked a hand to her chest. "You scared me. Why are you creeping around in the bushes?"

"Hoping to find something we missed last night, or my deputy missed this afternoon."

"Did you?" She wedged a fist on her hip.

"Just the mutt. Did he escape again?"

"He stuck around last night inside with no complaint, but the minute I set him free this morning, he took off. I'm hoping to lure him back with some more food tonight.

I bought him a bag of dog food and a dish. I also got a leash just in case he'll let me domesticate him for a trip to the vet."

"I think he's domesticated but scared of something. I heard him but couldn't get him to show himself."

Narrowing her eyes, she said, "How'd you know it was him?"

"Unless your attacker is panting and whining, my money's on the dog."

"Okay." She rolled her shoulders. "Do you want to help me bring the dog food inside? Then I'll have a look for an adapter for this card. I have it in my pocket. I can't believe the memory card would be literally at my feet, but what else could it be?"

"Could be lookie-loos taking videos of the Misty Hollow Massacre site. You don't even know how long it's been sitting there. We could've easily missed it last night in the dark."

She screwed up one side of her mouth. "Who's taking video with an old camcorder instead of a phone? I don't think there are that many devices around that still use the SD cards."

"SD?"

"Secure digital."

"They're still in use." He ducked into the back of the Jeep and hoisted a forty-pound bag of dog food over his shoulder. "Oof! You're expecting the stray to come and stick around for a while, I see."

"I hope so. Olly's been after me to get a dog. I've been putting it off, but if this guy's going to fall into my lap, it must be a sign."

He followed her up the porch and watched as she unlocked the dead bolt on top before sliding the key into the lock on the door handle. She bumped the solid door with her hip, and he anxiously peered over her shoulder into the cavernous living room.

Pointing toward a long door in the kitchen, she said, "You can put the dog food in the pantry for now. I'm going to my brother's office upstairs to see if I can find something to read this card."

West nudged open the pantry door with the toe of his shoe and heaved the bag to the floor. His gaze darted around the well-stocked shelves. Astrid could hole up in this house for weeks without going out, if she needed to. He shook his head. Nobody was going to lay siege to Astrid in her home. He had to stop worrying so much about her…and her son. This job wasn't some kind of redemption gig for him.

"Found it!" Astrid's voice carried down the stairs on a note of excitement.

West closed the pantry and strode into the living room just as she jumped off the last step, waving an adapter between two fingers.

"I knew Tate would have something. I can just insert this into my laptop and slip the card into the slot." She woke up her laptop on the kitchen island and shoved the adapter into a port on the side of her computer.

The laptop beeped in recognition of the device, and Astrid pulled the memory card from her pocket and thumbed it into the slot.

West held his breath as the blue circle spun on the display. He eked out a tiny puff when the drive appeared on the monitor. Astrid double-clicked the icon, and then double-clicked on the unnamed folder.

When the folder opened showing a blank space, they both physically deflated. Astrid stated the obvious. "There's nothing there. It's empty."

West swallowed his disappointment. "Could the contents have been deleted already?"

"I suppose." She closed it and clicked on it again with the same result.

He shouldn't be giving her false hope that this thing was over. That road would only lead to more danger. "Although I doubt someone would delete the video and then drop the memory card where you could find it."

"U-unless they wanted me to know they found it." She drew her bottom lip between her teeth.

"Because they're such great guys, and they don't want you to worry after they attacked you not once, but three times?" He squeezed her shoulder to soften the blow of his words. "Look, I'm not sure what that card was doing at Misty Hollow—probably just some kind of weird coincidence. We're getting closer every day to solving Chase Thompson's murder and when we do, the people behind the attacks on you will have more to worry about than drone footage that may or may not show them committing murder."

"Are you?" She crossed her arms and wedged her fists against her body. "Getting close to finding his killer?"

They didn't have any witnesses or clues, but they had a good idea about the motive. "We're almost certain this is a drug deal gone bad, given Chase's ties to the Discovery Bay narcotics trade. It's a matter of making our way up the chain of command. Every drug cartel, big and small, has its hit squad—the people who provide the muscle."

Astrid hunched her shoulders as if to ward off a chill,

even though they were inside her kitchen. "I'm aware of how it works."

He raised his eyebrows in anticipation. Was she going to tell him all about her ex and his involvement in the drug trade as a crooked cop?

He paused through an awkward silence. She still didn't trust him.

Rubbing his hands together, he said, "We know how it works, too. These people killed someone in the middle of the day on a beach, a known drug dealer, who'd recently gotten a new supplier. It won't be hard to track them down. They're not that smart—but they are vicious."

She snapped the lid of her laptop closed with a sigh. "Which is not good news for me. I wish I could just post a sign on my door and car stating that I don't have the damned card."

"And I'm sure their question would be, if you don't have it, who does? Where did it go?"

Tapping her toe on the tiled floor, she asked, "Did you search for it already in all the likely places?"

"I did." He shook his head. "Like looking for a particular grain of sand on the beach. The tide could've taken it out if it fell out there. If it fell out on the cliff or on Olly's way home, it could be anywhere—windblown, buried under debris, crushed into the road by a tire."

"Yeah, well, I'm sorry for your investigation, but I hope that's exactly what did happen, and I hope those goons figure it out before they come at me again. If I had it and watched it, I would've turned it over to the police already." She flicked a lock of hair over her shoulder. "Not too smart, these drug dealers."

"I concur." He smacked his palm on the counter. "I'm

going to let you get back to your evening. I won't stop searching for it, and you keep things locked up tight out here. Watch yourself going to and from your vehicle."

Astrid puffed up her cheeks and blew out a breath. "Thanks for coming over. I probably should've checked the card before I called you."

"I'm glad you called. If it were the memory card from the drone, I would've wanted to be in on the first look." He took a step toward the front door and hesitated. "You sure you're going to be okay here tonight? I can have a deputy cruise by a few times."

"If someone's in the area, sure, but I know how thin the ranks of the DFSD are. I don't want to take away from a real crime in progress." She brushed past him on the way to the front door. "I'll be fine. This is a good security system…when it's activated."

His arm buzzed where she skimmed it with her own, and he followed her to the entryway. She disarmed the security and swung open the door, peering at the flood-lit drive.

Stepping onto the porch, he said, "Don't go outside at night."

"Ugh." She shoved her hair out of her face and closed her eyes. "I thought I was done living like that."

The tingling in his arm reached his fingertips, and he reached out to trace the line of her jaw. As her lashes fluttered, he ran his thumb along her bottom lip and her mouth parted at his touch. He ducked his head, but the sharp whine of a dog startled them both, and they sprang apart.

She blinked rapidly. "H-he came back."

"Sounds like it." West stretched his lips into a smile. That dog had the worst timing—and the weirdest bark.

The sun had just set, and West squinted through the dusky glow to locate the direction of the dog's yelps and whines.

Astrid squeezed his biceps. "He sounds like he's hurt, doesn't he?"

"Sounds like something's wrong." West whistled through his teeth. "C'mon, boy."

With a stealthy creep, the dog emerged from the other side of the Jeep, out of the woods where West had spotted him before. His eyes glowed in the low light, and West coaxed him with a whistle into the brighter lights fanning from the house.

Astrid descended the two steps of the porch and crouched. "Come. Do you want to eat?"

The dog's ears pricked at the sound of Astrid's voice, and he loped toward her, his tail wagging stiffly, the fur on his back standing at attention.

West breathed out a soft sigh. "He looks okay."

"He has something in his mouth." Astrid snapped her fingers. "That's right. Come over here and show me what you have."

As the dog trotted into the light, Astrid gasped. "He has blood on his face and mouth. He *is* hurt."

"Be careful. He might snap at you."

"You wouldn't do that, would you?" She made kissing noises, and that dog was no dummy. He walked toward her, the light fur on his face stained red with either his blood or the blood of the unfortunate creature he had in his mouth.

"I think he might've killed something. Don't try to take it from his mouth. He might bite you."

"Me and him are like this, now." She crossed her fingers as she took the last few steps to meet the dog, still emitting strange, feral noises from the back of his throat.

Astrid cupped her palm beneath the dog's mouth, pink drool hanging from his jowls. "Let me see what you have. Drop it."

With a shake of his head, the dog opened its maw, releasing his treasure in the center of Astrid's hand.

Astrid screamed and jerked her hand back.

As the dog wagged his tail and grinned, West scrambled down the steps to gawk over Astrid's shoulder at the dog's prized possession.

Astrid covered her mouth. "I-is that a finger?"

West grabbed a stick and nudged the fleshy item. His gut twisted. "Yep. It's a finger with blue-chipped nail polish."

Chapter Eleven

Gagging, Astrid staggered to her feet and folded her arms across her stomach. "Where did he get that? It looks... fresh to me."

West swore under his breath. "I'm pretty sure I know whose finger that is and if I'm right, it's definitely fresh."

"You do?" Astrid jerked up her head while the dog whined, still looking for kudos. "How can you identify someone from a finger?"

"Because I was just talking to its owner—Chase Thompson's girlfriend. I noticed the blue fingernail polish. Of course, I could be wrong."

"Good boy." Astrid patted the dog on the head. "Then it's Naomi Wakefield's. I've seen them together when she's strung out."

"Yeah, I'd say that's most of the time." He blocked the dog from picking up finger and said, "Can you get me a plastic bag? We can't let this beast mutilate the finger anymore. It's evidence. Then I'm calling a team out here to search for her body."

Astrid stopped, one foot on the first step of the porch, and twisted her head around. "Body?"

"You don't think old Spot here up and ripped off Naomi's finger while she was living and breathing, do you?"

He nudged the dog with his knee and hovered protectively over the finger.

"I was kind of hoping that maybe she's injured, and the dog took advantage of her. I don't want to think about the rest." She spun around and pushed through the front door. On unsteady legs, she grabbed a plastic bag from a drawer in the kitchen.

If Chase's killers murdered Naomi Wakefield because they suspected her of passing information to West, would they ever give up on their assumption that she had the video from the drone? But if she did have it, she'd have already turned it over to West and if the footage did ID the killers, they'd be in trouble by now. They had to assume she didn't have it. Didn't they?

She gripped the edge of the counter with one hand, the other pinching the plastic bag between two fingers, and took a deep breath.

When she went back outside, she waved the baggie at West, on the phone and giving orders. He nodded his thanks and took the bag from her. He ended the call as he crouched down, a glove on one hand.

He shook open the baggie and picked up the dog's prize with two fingers. He dropped it in the bag and sealed it. "I have a couple of deputies coming out to do a search of the forest between where Naomi and I met and where she left her car. I'm assuming she was ambushed on her way to her vehicle."

"Why? Did Naomi tell you anything about Chase?"

"Not much." He scratched the dog on top of the head. "Except she did mention she suspected Chase had another girlfriend."

"Doesn't sound like much to me. Maybe they just didn't like her talking to you."

Driving two fingers into his temple, West said, "We were careful. Nobody knew we were meeting. I made sure nobody was following me, and I figured she'd do the same because she was paranoid about being seen with me."

"It's not your fault." She touched his forearm, braided with veins and tensile strength as he clenched his fist.

West's voice had taken on a strange quality—not quite guilt but maybe regret. Cops weren't generally responsible for the safety of witnesses, unless some kind of commitment had been made to testify. God knows, her ex didn't care what happened to his witnesses, but West appeared to be an entirely different breed of law enforcement officer—at least so far.

He squeezed his eyes closed for a brief second and then seemed to emerge from his funk. "I'm going to use the dog before the team gets here to see if he can lead me to the body. I don't want any more animals carrying off pieces of it."

A chill touched the back of Astrid's neck. "The drug trade on this island is getting ridiculous. Sheriff Hopkins turned a blind eye too many times because he didn't want to be bothered."

"Or he was afraid." West lifted one shoulder. "Let's go, boy."

The dog stood at attention and pointed with his nose at the forest. West held the bloody finger, now encased in plastic, in front of the dog's face, and the dog took a few tentative steps toward the tree line.

West followed, but the dog stopped and whined, pinning Astrid with a hopeful look.

She twisted her lips into a frown. "He wants me to come along."

"You don't have to. I can wait for the team if the dog doesn't want to lead me to Naomi. I'm sure it's not going to be pretty."

"I'll close my eyes." She pulled her sweater around her and joined West. "Let's go, Sherlock. Show us the body."

As Astrid joined West, the dog trotted ahead of them, his nose alternately to the ground and up in the air. She lengthened her stride to keep up with West and the dog, who now seemed like a heat-seeking missile.

They tromped deeper into the woods, and West tried to hold back branches for her as they veered off the beaten track.

Panting, she pointed through a thicket of trees. "The road is going to be visible pretty soon. Did you meet with her on the other side?"

"I did. I parked north of the road, and I believe she parked on this side. She probably would've been safer coming and going with me. Probably would've been safer at the station. But she insisted on the cloak-and-dagger stuff." West smacked at a bug on his arm. "She must've been followed. They probably had their eyes on her as soon as they killed Chase."

"Poor girl. I don't mean to speak ill of the dead, but Chase Thompson was bad news for everyone he touched. If he was cheating on Naomi with someone else, that woman had better watch her back, too."

"Naomi thinks Chase may have had a burner phone for his affair. We're going to have to thoroughly search their place."

"Thought you would've done that already." Astrid tripped over a root and grabbed for West's arm.

He steadied her with a hand on her back. "We did, but we'll go through it again. We didn't find a phone on his body, and we still haven't gotten the records from the phone company regarding his activity. We…"

The dog started barking furiously ahead of them, and West whistled to call him back.

"I appreciate his efforts, but we don't want the mutt disturbing the crime scene any more than he has."

Clutching her stomach with one hand and standing on her tiptoes, Astrid, asked, "You're sure he led us to her body? Maybe it's just body…parts that he found."

"One way to find out." He squeezed her shoulder. "You can stay here."

"I-I can't really at this point." Some hard core in her heart overcame her trepidation about seeing a dead body. If this crime was linked to her and that drone, she had to see with her own eyes what these people were capable of.

The dog appeared before them, his eyes gleaming, his nostrils flared.

Astrid touched the soft fur on his head. "Let's go."

"Me first." West stepped in front of her and picked his way over the forest bed, following the dog. He stopped suddenly and held his hand behind him. "It's exactly what we expected. You don't need to see it."

As West got on his phone, Astrid sat heavily on a fallen log and pulled her hood up and around her face. This was all way too close for comfort. How did she keep getting pulled into drug violence when she never even touched the stuff?

The dog sat beside her, thumping his tail against the

log, and she stroked his back. "You're a good boy, Sherlock. Are you going to protect me from these maniacs?"

"Sherlock." West joined her on the log. "Is that what you named him?"

"Seems fitting, doesn't it?" She tipped her head toward the small clearing where she still refused to look. "Don't you have to do something...over there?"

"The less I do right now, the better. Deputies were already on their way from when I called them before. I just called in the precise location, and they'll be arriving soon with a forensic kit. We need to collect some evidence in the area."

"H-how was she killed?" Astrid swallowed, and then tried to take in a full breath of pine-scented air.

"Same way as Chase—bullet to the head, execution style, but not before they did a little damage." West clenched his jaw, and a muscle twitched. "Looks like they wanted some information out of her. That finger Sherlock brought to us? Let's just say, he's not the one who detached it from Naomi's hand."

Astrid curled her own fingers into fists, as if to protect them. "Do you think that's what they have in store for me if I don't give up that memory card?"

"You don't have it."

"Exactly." She jerked her thumb toward the clearing. "She probably didn't have anything to give them, either. Didn't stop them from chopping bits off of her."

A siren whooped from the road on the other side of the clearing, and West pushed up to his feet, smacking dirt from the seat of his khaki uniform pants. "Time to get to work. I'll have one of the deputies walk you back to your place, or better yet, drive you and Sherlock back."

She'd been kind of hoping West would do those honors himself, but he had another murder investigation on his hands.

She stood up next to him on wobbly knees. If he noticed her nerves, he didn't call her out. "Okay, I'm going to get home and call my son before they turn in for the night or make s'mores or whatever they're doing out there. Some nice, normal activity that doesn't involve dead bodies and severed fingers."

A bright spotlight illuminated the area, and Astrid squinted at the figures emerging from the source. One called out. "Sheriff?"

"On the other side of the clearing. Be careful where you're stepping. I'll come to you." West turned to Astrid and ran his hands down her arms, ending with a light clasp of both her hands. "Lock up when you get home and invite Sherlock inside with you. Give him a reward for his hard work. Don't worry about what's going on out here. These murders are drug-related, and the perpetrators have to know that if you had video of Chase's murder from that drone, you would've turned it over by now. I'm confident they'll leave you alone and at the rate they're killing people, we'll catch them. Are you ready?"

"For?" She didn't move a muscle for fear that West would drop her hands.

"I'm going to walk you across the crime scene to the road. Keep your head averted."

She nodded, and he took her hand, leading her to the clearing. She kept her gaze pinned on the deputies gathered at the edge of the crime scene, just outside the yellow tape they'd strung between the trees.

With a wink just for her, West turned her over to a

young deputy with instructions to drive her and Sherlock back to her place and wait until they both went inside. The deputy discharged his duty faithfully, and Astrid marched straight to the kitchen after she'd barricaded herself inside the cabin.

"West is right. You deserve a reward and a clean up." She rubbed Sherlock's chest as she wiped the blood from his face with a wet rag. Then she went to the pantry to open the bag of dog food. She dumped a healthy amount into a bowl and added some water to it. As she set it down, he cocked his head at her. "Don't look at me that way. I'll give you some of my chicken, too."

Missing her son and her brother, Astrid kept up a one-sided conversation with Sherlock as she made a quick dinner for herself. She carried her plate of chicken and rice to the island and dropped a few pieces of meat into Sherlock's bowl. "Is that better, Sherlock?"

While she ate, she checked her phone for any information about Naomi Wakefield, but the media hadn't caught on yet. She pushed her plate away and called Porter Monroe's cell phone.

He picked up after the first ring, probably already fielding calls from anxious parents. "Hello, Astrid."

"Hi, Porter. Everything good?"

"Yeah, the kids seem to be having a good time…"

She caught her breath at his pause. "But?"

"No, no. Olly's fine. Went fishing today and caught a few for lunch. The boys went swimming in the lake, and we had inner tubes for the river. Good times."

"You sort of hesitated at the end. Is something going on?" She tried to steady her breathing. Olly was safe and having fun.

"Olly seems out of sorts—nothing serious, nothing like depression or anything like that. No acting out. Just a little quieter than I'm used to seeing him."

Astrid chewed on her bottom lip. "Could be, you know, things with his father."

"I'm aware of the situation and figured his subdued demeanor might be the result of that." Porter huffed out a big breath. "Do you want to speak with him? He won't be singled out. Quite a few of the boys have already talked to their parents."

"Sure, if he wants to talk to me."

"Hang on."

Astrid jiggled her leg up and down while she waited through the silence. She whispered to Sherlock. "Maybe I should tell him about you to lift his spirits."

"Hey, Mom."

"Hi, Olly. Heard you caught some fish today." Even she could hear the false brightness of her tone. She grimaced at Sherlock.

"Yeah, it was a good spot. We cleaned 'em and ate 'em, too."

"Sounds yum." She cleared her throat. "Are you having fun?"

"Yeah, sure. Almost all my friends are here, except Ryan. He had to visit his grandparents in like Idaho or someplace."

"I'm sure he's having fun, too." Did Olly's tone sound flat? Tense? Or had Porter just put that idea in her head? She stared at Sherlock for a second.

"D-did you get that drone to work?"

Astrid bit her bottom lip. It wasn't like Olly to obsess over something he did wrong or bring it up. He usually tried to sweep that sort of thing under the rug. She had no intention of telling him that someone stole the drone from Jimmy's Auto.

"No. Davia's not going to bother. She wanted a newer, shinier model, anyway." She drummed her fingers on the counter. "That still doesn't mean you're off the hook, bud. I'm thinking you should do a little cleanup around the office when you get back—empty trash, do some shredding, whatever Davia needs."

"Okay. I can do that." The raised voices of kids almost drowned out his final words. "Gotta go, Mom."

He ended the call before she could respond or ask to speak to Porter. She tapped the cell phone against her chin. "That whole break-in must've upset him more than he let on, Sherlock. Don't know why he's so interested in that drone. Wish he'd stop asking about it, so I don't have to keep lying."

The phone buzzed in her hand, and she tapped it. "Did you forget something? Like, love you, Mom? Miss you?"

The silence on the other end of the line caused a cold ripple along her spine, and she pulled the phone away from her ear to check the calling number—not Porter's, unknown.

She licked her dry lips. "Hello?"

A woman's voice, both hushed and gravelly at the same time, answered. "We know you probably don't have the memory card from the drone, Astrid, but if you find it before we do and turn it over to that sheriff, you're going to suffer more than that junkie Naomi did, more than your traitorous ex will when we find him. By the way, where's Olly?"

Chapter Twelve

A fist squeezed her heart, and Astrid almost tipped off the stool. Gripping the edge of the island, she growled, "None of your damned business. You people must know by now I don't have the drone's memory card."

The woman hissed like a cat. "Because you would've turned it over to the sheriff by now. But you're looking for it, aren't you?"

"No. Th-the only reason I wanted to find it at first was to hand it over to you. I don't care about Chase Thompson. I don't care about your activities. And I don't care for law enforcement." Astrid locked her jaw. At least that's how she felt before Sheriff West Chandler landed on the island with his hot bod and hazel eyes and do-gooder spirit.

The woman clicked her tongue. "The amount of time you're spending with the sheriff puts a lie to that."

"That's because you've been stalking and attacking me. What do you want me to do? I told your…colleague the other night I didn't have it and didn't know where it was."

"You know what else tells me you're lying, Astrid?"

Astrid swallowed against a throat that felt like sandpaper. She managed to croak one word. "What?"

"When you did find a memory card, you ran right to the sheriff. You didn't hide it or destroy it. You called your buddy, Sheriff Chandler, to turn it over to him."

The knots twisting in Astrid's gut tightened. "I-I...did you plant that there to test me?"

"You failed." The woman's voice dropped, and she whispered. "Don't fail again."

Before Astrid could make an excuse or assure the woman she had no interest in the drone footage, her tormentor ended the call.

Astrid jumped from the stool, startling Sherlock. She cruised to every door and window in the place to double-check the locks and pull the drapes tight. They were watching her. They knew everything she'd been doing. Now they knew Olly's name and the fact that he was gone.

How long would it take them to find out where he was? A friendly woman pretending to have a son of her own asking about activities? There were enough tourists on the island for the spring holiday that someone like that could blend in with the rest.

Why had she mentioned Russ? Were these the same people who had been involved in her ex's case? The drug trade was a small network, just like any other profession. They probably knew each other. Were they actively trying to find Russ? She couldn't help them with that, either.

After checking her security system, she sank to the kitchen floor next to Sherlock, where he'd fallen asleep next to his bowl. They'd only want to get to Olly to punish her. She wouldn't give them any reason to do that.

She'd stop looking for the drone. She'd stop looking for that memory card. And she'd stop seeing West Chandler.

THE MORNING AFTER Astrid's stray found Naomi Wakefield's dead body, West woke up with a racing heart and a pounding headache. He stuffed some pillows behind his back, closed his eyes and took several deep breaths.

When the guilt tried to worm its way into his brain, he tried to shift his thoughts to all the people he'd helped throughout his career—at least that's what his therapist told him to do. He had the scenarios lined up in his head—saved a baby from a burning car, talked a husband out of slicing his wife's throat, foiled a gangbanger's hit on his teenage witness.

Those scenes marched through his brain, behind his closed eyes. But why did they always end with a dead four-teen-year-old holding an unloaded gun? Would Naomi's lifeless body join that image in his nightmares?

West cursed and rolled out of bed, tripping over a box. He had to spend a day unpacking and getting his rental house sorted out. He couldn't live out of boxes forever.

As he made his way to the kitchen to prepare some breakfast, he glanced at his phone. He'd had a late night at the crime scene and didn't want to disturb Astrid when he'd finished. He breathed easier when he didn't see any messages or phone calls from her. Everything must've been quiet at her place last night.

He'd resume his search for the drone's memory card, but he knew anything could've happened to it by now. Maybe a bird carried it away and tucked it into a new nest.

He cracked some eggs into a pan and turned on the heat. As he pushed the eggs around, he scrolled through his phone with his thumb. He nearly dropped his phone into the pan of eggs when he saw a text message from Naomi. How'd that happen? They'd found her phone in her pocket last night and as far as he knew, it was safely checked in to evidence. Nobody in the department would play a joke like that.

He turned off the eggs and tapped the message to read it. She'd texted him a name—Monique. Could that be Chase's chick on the side? The date and time stamp on the message showed today's date about ten minutes ago.

He made a quick call to the station to make sure that Naomi's cell phone had been checked into evidence and waited while the deputy on-call looked to verify it was still there. West let out the breath he was holding when the deputy returned with the good news.

Naomi's phone was password protected, so they'd turned it off. They'd let tech handle getting into the phone, but this message made that task even more urgent. Naomi must've put that message on a timer or something. Had she planned to clear out of town before Chase's killers could make the connection between her and their information about Monique?

He dumped the eggs onto a plate and forked big clumps into his mouth as he hunched over the counter. He washed it all down with a few gulps from the orange juice container.

He showered and dressed in his uniform in record time and hit the road to the station, which sat a little outside of the town. He would've expected the sheriff's station to be smack-dab in the middle of the main drag, but it occupied some prime real estate instead. A savvy sheriff in the past had some odd priorities—maybe that was before the drug trade hit Discovery Bay hard, and the deputies were still dealing with cats up trees and fights between neighbors. The good old days.

By the time he reached the station, he was craving caffeine and stopped at the coffee pot on his way to his office without even putting down his bag.

"Late night?" Deputy Robard raised her eyebrows at him.

"Chase Thompson's girlfriend, Naomi Wakefield."

"I heard." She shook her head. "You know that saying— lie with dogs, get fleas, or something like that. Chase was a dog."

"Yeah, Naomi was in a bad way when I talked to her." West dumped some vanilla creamer in his coffee and swirled it with a stir stick.

"Did she at least give you anything? They must've been worried that she would or did, but you'd think they would've killed her *before* she talked to you, not after."

"She didn't give me anything at the time, except the suspicion that Chase had another girlfriend. She couldn't tell me a name, but she gave it to me later, after she died." West patted his front pocket where he'd stashed his phone.

Robard's eyes popped open. "How'd she do that?"

"Text message."

"Before she died?"

"After."

"What the..." Robards took a gulp of her own coffee. "That's some voodoo right there."

"I think she sent the text on a time delay." He leveled a finger at her. "Don't you work tech?"

"In a pinch. Discovery Bay hosts a tech unit for all the islands, but I've been to the training."

"Perfect." He jerked his thumb toward the hallway. "Do you think you can get into Naomi's phone and find out if that's what happened? I don't want to assume the message is from her if it isn't. Could be someone else trying to trick us, send us down the wrong path."

Rubbing her hands together, she said, "Phone hacking. One of my favorite things to do."

"Go ahead and check it out of evidence and have a look. I'm mostly interested in if she delayed sending that message to me, but of course, have a look at her other messages, too. I'd be interested in her communications with Chase before he was murdered. We never found his phone, and his carrier hasn't sent us his records yet."

"Yeah, that always seems to take a while around here. I'll get right on that, sir."

West carried his coffee into his office and logged in to his computer. He pulled out his cell phone and dropped it on his desk. Still nothing from Astrid. A buzz of apprehension flitted in his ear, so he texted her. She'd been the victim of several attacks this week. Why wouldn't he check up on her?

He watched the message until it showed *delivered*, and then continued watching for a response. He sat up in his chair when he saw the three little dots flicker on his display. They disappeared. Reappeared. Disappeared again.

Huffing out a breath through his nose, he turned to his computer. She probably had a lot on her plate today if she planned to take in Sherlock. He hoped she would. That dog showed some real smarts last night and seemed to have bonded with Astrid already.

A few minutes later, Deputy Robard popped her head in his office, holding up Naomi's cell phone in its leopard-print case between her gloved fingers. "Got it, boss. I'll give it a whirl and let you know what I find."

"Thanks, Robard."

She cocked her head. "You can call me Amanda, boss."

"Right, Amanda. Thanks."

He'd have to get used to working in a smaller department where he'd be dealing with the same deputies every day on every case.

He spent the next thirty minutes reviewing the ballistics reports from Chase's and Naomi's murders. Same weapon had done them both, but Chase's murder had been more clinical, more businesslike. Naomi's had seemed more personal. Could she have known her killer? Maybe the murderer was just hell-bent on taking a little revenge because Naomi had spoken to him.

As he stretched his arms over his head and eyed the dregs of his coffee, Amanda tapped on his open door. Her bright eyes signaled good news.

"You got in?"

"I did." She tipped the phone back and forth. "She did a delayed send on that message to you. So that was her, for sure. Not much between her and Chase in the days leading up to his murder, but I'll type up a transcript, so you can go over it yourself."

"Good work, Amanda. I'm going to start looking for this Monique. Chase may have been keeping her a secret from Naomi for obvious reasons, but his friends might know something more about her. Unless Naomi timed another delayed text message to me with more information, the name is all I got."

"You've been to the Salty Crab?" Amanda wrinkled her nose as she said the name of the dive bar. "That was Chase's hangout. If Dead Falls Island has a wrong side of the tracks, it's all centered at the Crab."

"Yeah, I've had the pleasure, and it's my first stop.

The medical examiner hasn't performed a postmortem on Naomi yet, so I have time this afternoon." He grabbed his jacket from the hook behind his desk. "Let me know if you find out anything else of interest on Naomi's phone about Chase's activities or this other woman."

"Will do, boss."

He pushed to his feet behind his desk. "Uh, you can call me West."

"I'll stick with boss, for now." She gave him a mock salute.

He smiled to himself as he grabbed the keys to his SUV. The DFSD had gotten a bad rap under its previous sheriff, but he'd found nothing but dedicated, hardworking deputies so far. He planned to start with Chase's murder and clean up the drug trade on this island. Its proximity to the Canadian border had made it a hub for drug trafficking between the two countries, but he was determined to shut it down.

He drove into town and parked down the street from the Salty Crab. He didn't want to drive away business from the bar by taking up residence there. As he walked to the Crab, he glanced at his phone, and his stomach did a little dive when he saw no response from Astrid.

When he entered the bar, he blinked several times to adjust to the darkness. The bartender stood out, illuminated by the neon signs behind him flashing off the mirror, and he crossed his beefy, tattooed arms when he caught sight of West by the door. Different guy from the one the other night, who'd brought him towels for Astrid.

He was hoping the same bartender would be working, but maybe this one would be as helpful as the other guy. West bellied up to the bar, a few stools down from the only other patron seated there, and rapped his knuckles on the sticky wood top. "Coke, please."

The pumped-up guy swiped a wet cloth across the bar in front of West and tossed down a cardboard coaster, advertising a local brew. "I know you don't just wanna Coke. You got something to ask me about Naomi?"

West tipped his head. "What's your name?"

"Jackson Cross, and Naomi was a regular here along with her old man, Chase. The two of them…" He shook his head, his shaggy hair brushing his shoulders.

West asked, "Trouble?"

"Everyone knew Chase was dealing." Jackson held up both calloused hands. "But not in here, man. I wouldn't allow it. I had to keep riding him to take his business outside. Naomi wasn't much better." Jackson crossed himself and kissed a heavy cross dangling against his chest, along with several other chains. "RIP."

"Do you know if Chase was cheating on Naomi? Seeing another woman?"

Jackson selected a glass from a tray, scooped some ice into it and shot a steady stream of soda into it from a nozzle. He set it down on the coaster and dropped a straw on the bar next to it. "Can't say for sure. He could've had a couple of side chicks. You know when a guy's carrying product like that, the ladies who are that way inclined come running."

"Was someone named Monique one of those ladies?" West took a sip of his Coke, watching Jackson over the rim. The bartender's face didn't change.

"Monique? Doesn't ring a bell." Jackson scratched at his beard.

"I know Monique." The man sitting to West's right, hunched over a beer, turned his head.

As Jackson wandered off to help a customer waving him down at the end of the bar, West turned to fully face the skinny man next to him, slumped over the bar. "What's your name?"

The man shoved a mess of greasy blond hair behind one ear. "Benji Duran."

Benji didn't offer his hand, still wrapped around his sweating mug, so West kept his resting on his thigh. One quick move or one strong gust of wind, and this guy might topple over. "Benji, I'm Sheriff Chandler."

"I know who you are." Benji took a gulp of beer and wiped the foam from his mouth with the back of his hand. "You gonna find out who killed Chase and Naomi?"

"We're working on it." West took another sip of his drink. Benji didn't seem like a man you rushed. "So, you know Monique?"

"Oui, oui." Benji snorted at his own cleverness, and a fizz of beer bubbled from his left nostril.

West pulled his gaze away from Benji's red-tipped nose and focused on his watery blue eyes. "Is Monique really French, or are you just riffing on her name?"

"Naw, she's French. She's got a French accent and all. French Canadian." Benji grabbed a cocktail napkin and blew his nose.

Had he been one of Chase's customers or was booze his particular poison? Could he trust what came out of Benji's mouth? If he hoped to get anything out of Benji, he'd have to be specific.

"Did Monique hang out with Chase?"

"Yeah. Chase got all the fine ladies."

"Is Monique still here on Dead Falls Island?"

"I think so. I saw her yesterday."

West did the calculation in his head as he tipped his glass again. Monique was here a few days after Chase's murder. "Where did you see her? Does she come here to the Salty Crab?"

Benji shook his head and finished off his beer. Tapping the side of his glass, he asked, "You buying?"

"Jackson." West held up his hand in the air. "Another brewski for my man Benji."

West had to bite his tongue while Jackson swept Benji's empty mug from the table and replaced it with a fresh, frosty one, topped with foam, with Benji watching his every move with rapt attention, his tongue lodged in the corner of his mouth.

With his new beer in front of him, Benji closed his eyes and took a sip.

Benji's craving satisfied, West cleared his throat. "So, did you see Monique here at the Crab?"

"She never comes here."

West ground his back teeth. "Is that because Chase came here with Naomi?"

"Monique was too good for this dive." Benji flicked a hand dismissively at his surroundings. "She made Benji take her to the Harbor Restaurant and Bar where she drank dack…dack…" Benji gave up and took another slug of beer.

"Daiquiris?"

Benji tried to snap his fingers and failed. "Thas right."

"Is that where you last saw Monique? The Harbor?"

"I don't go in there. Overpriced beer."

West took a deep breath. "Where'd you see her, Benji? Do you know where she stays on the island?"

"Saw her on the street, man. Just walking. Tried to say hey, but she acted like she didn't know me."

"What does she look like?"

"Fine."

West rolled his eyes at Jackson, hovering nearby, and the bartender took pity on West.

Jackson smacked his dish towel next to Benji's drink, making Benji jump in his seat. "Benji, is Monique that black-haired woman who smokes those cigarettes with a cigarette holder? Calls everyone *mon cher* or some crap like that?"

Benji's chin dropped to his sunken chest. "Never called *me* that."

Jackson plowed on with more patience than West possessed. "That's her though, right? Long black hair. Wears that little rabbit fur jacket? Smokes like a chimney."

Benji mumbled. "That's Monique."

West mouthed a thank-you to Jackson, who shrugged.

"Dude's been coming in here for years. You eventually figure out how to talk to him once he's a few sheets to the wind." Jackson tugged on his beard. "So, I have seen her around. Just didn't know her name was Monique, and I never saw her with Chase. Didn't seem his type, but I suppose she was slumming to cozy up to our local dealer. She must have a bad habit. Can't tell you where she stays, though. I've just seen her around."

"Thanks for your help, Jackson." West dropped some bills on the bar to cover his soda and a few of Benji's beers. "Now I'll shove off and stop scaring away your clientele."

Back outside, West rubbed his eyes. All he had to do was search for a black-haired, chain-smoking, daiquiri-drinking fox named Monique…and try to run into her on the street.

As he loped back to his vehicle, he caught sight of a blond-haired fox instead, coming out of the local pet store.

Waving his hand to catch Astrid's attention, he veered to the left, making a beeline for where she stood on the sidewalk, outside the store.

Sensing his approach, her head jerked up. Her eyes widened in her face…and then she turned and ran.

Chapter Thirteen

Oh, damn. Oh, damn. What was *he* doing here? And in the middle of town, in the middle of the day where anyone could see them. She careened around the next corner, the plastic bag from the pet store hitting her leg. Feeling like a character in a chase film, she ducked into a souvenir shop.

She took up a position behind a carousel of magnets sporting the falls, the bay and the lighthouse, peering around the edge at the window. When West's solid frame strode past the glass, she crouched.

The clerk came from behind the counter, twisting her pink-tinged hair around one finger. "Can I help you?"

"No, ah, yes." Astrid peeled a magnet from the display and held it up. "I'll take this one."

"Okay, whatever." The young woman shuffled back to the counter and rang up Astrid's purchase.

Before leaving the store, Astrid poked her head into the street, scanning the sidewalk, right and left. Okay, this was ridiculous. She couldn't hide from the sheriff forever, could she?

She dropped the magnet into the bag with Sherlock's toys and chews and walked into the nearest coffeehouse. She snagged a seat by the window and pulled out her phone. She finally answered West's most recent text with a message to meet her at Tate's boat in the harbor in fifteen minutes, and she'd explain everything then. Would she? Could she?

She ordered a latte, and then sat by the window watching her phone's display. She wouldn't blame him if he blew her off. After everything he did for her, she turned and ran when she saw him. What would've happened last night if Sherlock hadn't interrupted their kiss? Because that *was* gonna be a kiss. Maybe that's why he thought she turned tail and scurried away—maybe that's why she should've.

West's answer came through at the same time the barista announced her latte. He'd meet her in thirty. She texted him quick directions and a smiley emoji to take away the sting of her flight.

Fifteen minutes later, she dumped her empty coffee cup in the trash can and headed toward the marina. She pulled into a parking space at the edge of the lot and shoved her bag under the seat. As she slid from her truck, she flipped up her hoodie and kept her head down.

She entered the gate to the boat slips, and her rubber-soled shoes smacked against the metal gangplank as she made a beeline for Tate's boat, *Fire Dancer*. She prepared the boat for launch by checking the bilge plug, pulling up the fenders and shoving the key in the ignition. Now she just needed her passenger.

She didn't have to wait long. A few minutes later, West strode down the ramp, the breeze lifting his dark hair above his sunglasses. When he spotted her on the boat, his gait slowed. He reached the slip and pointed at her. "Do you need the secret code word now?"

"There is no code word. Hop on." She turned on the engine, and the boat purred in the water.

Cocking his head, he said, "We're actually going out to sea? Are you going to dump my body overboard when you're finished with me?"

"Don't be ridiculous. You game, or no?" She patted the edge of the *Fire Dancer*.

"I'm in." He stepped onto the boat and sat on a cushion next to the motor. "Seriously, I don't have time for a pleasure cruise."

"This is business, not pleasure, Sheriff." She eased on the throttle and backed out of the slip. Then she swung the boat around and chugged into the sea lane.

Once they hit a rhythm, West turned from the bay to face her. "Why all the cloak-and-dagger stuff, and why did you run away from me in town?"

"I got a phone call last night after you left."

"Oh?" He shoved his sunglasses on top of his head.

"It was a woman warning me to stop looking for the drone's memory card."

"So, they've come to the conclusion you don't have it and don't know where it is."

"They figured I would've turned it over to you by now if I had it." She caught her hair in her hand as it blew across her face. "But they're watching me. They seem to know my every move."

He rubbed his knuckles against his clean-shaven jaw. "We figured that much. They know your truck. They know where you live and work."

"It's worse than that." Astrid waved to another boater as she tipped the steering wheel to the right to enter the open bay. "They planted that blank memory card at the Misty Hollow property as a test. I failed."

"How so?" West sat up straighter.

"They know I turned it over to you." She lifted her shoulders as a cool breeze blew through her. "They know more than my home and car. They're spying on me."

"What did you tell her?"

She widened her eyes. "What did you want me to say? I told her I was done looking for that card. That I didn't care what had happened to Chase Thompson."

Snapping his fingers, he said, "That's why you ran from me? It's not my breath or my aftershave?"

Should she tell him now, he always smelled great? And she knew for a fact he didn't mask his own natural, masculine scent with aftershave. Russ used to bathe in the stuff, and it made her gag—even before he turned into a criminal.

She nodded mutely. "I-I just figured it would look better if I weren't living in your pocket."

His eyebrows shot up to his hairline. "You've been living in my pocket? What does that even mean?"

"We *have* been spending a lot of time together." She dropped her lashes and hoped he'd mistake the pink in her cheeks for the wind.

"Because they keep making you a victim of their attacks."

"That's what I told her. I asked her if she expected me not to report the attacks against me to the sheriff."

"Did you mollify her?"

"I'm not sure." Astrid bit her bottom lip. "She made some veiled threats against Olly."

"She would. They would. They always threaten those you love most."

The boat hit a small wave, and a shimmer of water sprayed West. Sparkling droplets clung to the ends of his hair and his eyelashes. He dropped his glasses over his eyes again and licked the salt from his lips.

"I agree with her…and you. Stop taking any measures to find the drone, fix it or look for its missing parts. You don't need to be a part of this. It was just bad timing that Olly took the drone and flew it near the scene of a murder."

"Okay." Her hands rested lightly on the steering wheel. "Should I stop, I mean, should we stop seeing each other in public?"

With his head turned back toward the bay, he seemed not to have heard her. Suddenly, he whipped his head around. "This woman who called, what did she sound like?"

"She disguised her voice somewhat. She sounded gravelly, then whispery. I don't know if she was trying to sound threatening, or what, but I probably wouldn't recognize her voice if I heard her talking normally." She flicked a hand in the air. "And don't ask about a phone number. The call came up as an unknown number and when I tried to do a callback, it was blocked. I'm sure she's using a burner phone, so she can't be traced."

"Yeah, I'm sure she's just one of the drug cartel's many drones, excuse the pun, who goes out there and does what she's told. They probably used a woman to keep you off-balance."

"There was one thing weird about her speech." Astrid cut the speed on the boat and launched into a wide U-turn. "The way she pronounced my name."

"How'd she pronounce your name?"

"Well, the second syllable is a short *I* sound, and the accent is on the first syllable. She put the accent on the second syllable, and she mangled it by pronouncing the *I* like a long *E* sound. Like you'd pronounce an *I* in Spanish."

"Or French." West hit the boat's railing with his palm. "Could she have had a French accent?"

"Maybe. Why?"

"Chase Thompson's side chick was a French woman named Monique. From her description, she doesn't sound like Chase's type or vice versa. I was wondering what she'd be doing with a guy like Chase and figured it was his access to drugs. But…" Chase rubbed his jaw.

"But now you think it was to keep an eye on him." Astrid shifted the tiller to point the boat toward the entrance to the sea lane. "This Monique discovered Chase was skimming or stealing or whatever he was doing, she ratted him out to the big boss and set him up for murder."

"Could be."

"Have you met her yet?"

"Nobody knows where she's staying or even if she lives here permanently. I have a description and a possible hangout for her."

"What's the hangout?"

"The Harbor Restaurant and Bar. Must be around here, since we're at the harbor. Logical conclusion." West tapped his head.

Tilting her head back, Astrid pointed to the bluff above the harbor. "It's right up there. If she's sitting at her favorite bar, she could've looked right out the window and seen us together."

West came up behind her and reached over her shoulder, covering her hand with his. "There's no reason why we can't be seen together, Astrid. Just because we're a…couple, it doesn't mean you're actively looking for the drone footage or helping me in any way with that case."

She twisted her head over her shoulder and narrowed her eyes. "We're a couple? Since when?"

"Since now." Wedging a finger against her chin, he planted a salty kiss on her mouth.

Her knees almost buckled, and it had nothing to do with being on the deck of a boat. She let out a small gasp when he ended the kiss.

"Let's hope Monique and everyone else saw that." His soft lips, which had recently been caressing hers, quirked into a smile.

"So, you're suggesting we play at being a real couple so that everyone, including Monique and her cohorts, will assume what we have is personal instead of professional?"

"Something like that. Even though I'm the sheriff of Dead Falls Island, I'm allowed to have relationships and… friends."

"Well, then let's make sure everyone knows." She set the tiller on course and pivoted on her tiptoes, hooking one arm around West's waist.

He took the hint and bent his head to solidify their standing as a new couple by kissing her again. This one felt less showmance and more romance, but he could be a damned good actor.

He broke away and put his hand on the tiller. "Whoa, steady. You don't want to plow your brother's boat into the rocks."

"That would be even more convincing." She took over the steering and reduced the speed of the boat, although her heart had picked up the pace to make up for it.

"To launch our new status, I propose dinner tonight." He leveled a finger at the glass wall of the Harbor Restaurant. "Up there. And if Monique is there, even better. Let her see us enjoying a night out that has nothing to do with the drone or Chase's and Naomi's murders."

Combing her fingers through her tangled hair, Astrid asked, "And if Monique isn't there?"

West shrugged and winked. "The show must go on."

ASTRID HAD NO intention of telling Sam that all the fuss was for a fake date.

Sam squealed over their FaceTime call. "Wear the white silk blouse. With your blond hair, you always look like an ice queen in white."

Astrid held up the blouse under her chin and frowned into the mirror. "Do I want to look like an ice queen? Don't I want to look smokin' hot, instead?"

"What? And give him the impression that you're easy? You haven't done this for a while. Trust me." Sam took a sip of her wine.

"You've been separated for about four months now. How are you the expert?" Astrid slipped the blouse from the hanger and pulled it over her head, luxuriating in the softness against her skin.

"I read stuff." Sam shoved her hand into a bag of chips and crunched one between her perfect white teeth. "You're really taking advantage of your time with Olly gone. I can't wait until the Girl Scouts take their trip this summer—not that I won't miss Peyton. Do you miss Olly?"

"Of course. I'm going to give him a call before I go out. For some reason, he's kind of needy this trip. Wants to talk to me every night. I'm not complaining." Astrid dipped and hooked her fingers around the straps of a pair of high-heeled black sandals. "What do you think?"

"Killer." Sam licked her fingers. "But you'll be about six one in those. How tall is our hunky sheriff?"

"About that, I think. He's not the type to worry if a woman is taller than he is. He has more confidence than that."

"Unlike Russ." Sam covered her mouth with her greasy fingers. "Oops, sorry. Didn't mean to bring up bad juju before your first date in years."

"Doesn't bother me." Astrid sat on the edge of her bed and slipped her feet into the sandals. "Okay, I gotta go put some makeup on and give Olly that call before I leave."

"He's not picking you up?"

"I insisted we meet there. He'd have to double back."

"If you're driving, you can't get your drink on and invite him inside when he drops you off." Sam swirled her own wine before taking a gulp.

"I don't want to get tipsy, and I thought I was the ice queen."

Sam rolled her eyes. "You're the ice queen until he melts your core."

"You need to put away the trashy mags."

"All the trash is online now." Sam smoothed out the empty chip bag. "Seriously, though. If this date goes well, you should make sure West is okay with kids. I mean, after what he went through, maybe he's skittish about them."

Astrid dropped her makeup bag on the bed. "What are you talking about? What did he go through?"

"Wait. You've gone this far with him and haven't even done a search on him. Even *I* did a search on him, and I'm not even interested in dating him."

"You did a search on the sheriff?" The silky material of Astrid's blouse trembled as her heart pounded in her chest. "What did you discover?"

"Oh, Astrid. This is not the time to be telling you, right before a date with the man."

"You'd better spill it, Sam. What did you find out about West?"

"Oh, sister, he shot and killed a teenage boy."

Chapter Fourteen

Astrid's stomach dropped, and she clapped a hand over her mouth. "N-not on purpose. I mean, obviously not, or he'd be in prison. What happened?"

"It was some gang initiation thing where this teen had randomly shot into a crowd, hitting a toddler. When West went to apprehend the suspect, the kid pulled a gun on him. West shot him. Self-defense, right? That was the conclusion of the investigation. There were witnesses and everything."

"That's horrible for everyone." Astrid blinked back tears.

"What's worse is the gun the teen had was actually unloaded." She waved her hand. "Not that West could've known that."

Astrid shook her head. "What a tragic situation. Did the toddler die, too?"

"No, thank God, but West left the force after that."

"He must've been messed up." No wonder West seemed to bolt every time he saw Olly.

"Look, I'm sorry to be a downer. It wasn't West's fault, but he might have some lingering issues with preteen boys."

Astrid reached for her dresser and snatched up a tissue. She dabbed her nose. "I guess that's why he wanted to leave Chicago."

"Probably. I'll let you go. Bruce is calling tonight to set up a dinner to discuss reconciliation."

"And I'm all for it." Astrid aimed a kiss at the screen. "I'll talk to you later."

"Bye, girl."

Astrid sat on the bed, her makeup bag in her lap. Why hadn't West told her about his past? Maybe for the same reason she hadn't told him about hers. Had he already done a search on her like Sam did on him?

She slid off the end of the bed and leaned toward the mirror to apply her makeup. Then she navigated the stairs in her high heels, holding on to the banister. When she reached the kitchen, she placed a call to Porter's cell phone.

"Hello, Astrid. Perfect timing. I just sent the boys to wash up before helping with dinner. I'll get Olly for you."

Astrid backed up from Sherlock's nose. "Do not get my slacks dirty. I'll feed you before I go out."

"Hey, Mom."

"Hi. What did you do today?" She still hadn't told Olly about finding Sherlock again and feeding him, just in case the dog ran off, even though the vet assured her this morning he wasn't chipped.

Olly went into his typical recitation of events, bouncing from one topic to the next, usually with no timeline, rhyme or reason. She smiled as she listened to her son's scattered narrative.

As their conversation wound down and Olly started making noises about helping to clean the fish, he blurted out, "Did you fix the drone?"

She pursed her lips. "Olly, I told you not to worry about that. Davia is getting a new one from the company. Did the break-in at our house bother you? You can tell me. You can tell me anything, Olly. I-I know you've been through a lot with your dad."

Some noises from the background floated across the line, and Olly hiccupped. "I gotta go, Mom."

"Olly…"

Porter's voice interrupted her. "It's me, Astrid. Olly went outside to clean fish."

"Is he doing okay, Porter?"

"He's fine. Coming out of his shell a little, back to himself."

"Okay, I'll let you get to it."

She fed Sherlock, and then let him outside for the night wearing his new collar and tag. She'd eventually figure out a dog door situation, but not while she might still be the target of murdering drug dealers. She just had to hope Sherlock would stick around…and not bring home any more body parts.

She locked up the cabin and set off for her first date in years—even if West *had* asked her out to throw off the bad guys. A smile played across her lips. His ploy to get her to go out with him had to be one of the most creative she'd ever heard.

With parking at a premium on the bluff overlooking Dead Falls Harbor, Astrid left her truck with the lone valet parking attendant. She didn't even know what kind of car West drove outside of his DFSD SUV, so she had no clue if she beat him to the restaurant.

A flutter of apprehension skirted across her skin as she pulled open the door to the restaurant. If Monique was at her favorite bar tonight and saw her with West, what would the woman make of it? It's not like they'd be here to search for the drone or its memory card. Would it set Monique's mind at ease to think Astrid and West had other reasons to hook up...hang out? Or would it make her more concerned?

As Astrid approached the hostess table, West hopped off a barstool and intercepted her.

"I told the waitress I'd wait for you before taking our table. The busboy had to clean it off, anyway."

"It should be ready now, Sheriff Chandler." The pretty hostess in the slinky black dress batted her eyelashes at West.

Astrid held her breath, but West didn't seem to notice except to smile at the woman and thank her. Russ would've turned on the charm by this point and ended the evening with the woman's phone number in his pocket. Astrid gave her head a little shake. Not all cops were slick Romeos... but they all seemed to have secrets.

The hostess showed them to a table by the window, and the lights from the harbor twinkled, reflecting off the water, giving the whole scene an impressionist haziness.

West pulled out her chair. "Unless you prefer the other side of the table."

"This is fine." When the hostess left them, Astrid hunched forward, elbows on the table. "Did you spot the French woman in the bar?"

"I did not."

"So, without the appropriate audience, maybe we should wrap this up early."

West shook his head. "Where's your patience? She could show up at any time."

Through an appetizer of calamari, a beer for West and a strawberry daiquiri for her, the main course and a shared tiramisu, Monique still hadn't made an appearance, but several heads had turned their way, guaranteeing a mention in the Dead Falls gossip mill.

By the end of the evening, Astrid discovered that West had been engaged once but never married. He left his job as a police officer in Chicago due to stress, but he left the story hanging. It wasn't her place to chime in now. When she realized he had no intention of finishing it, she checked her phone. "Probably should call it a night, huh?"

"Mission accomplished." West leaned back in his chair and shook the ice in his water glass.

"I know." She cupped a hand around her mouth. "We got all the tongues wagging."

"That's not what I meant." His hazel eyes shifted to a deep green in the candlelight. "I'd been wanting to get to know you better since the day I met you at the Spring Fling—away from the danger and the threats and the fear. Like I said, mission accomplished."

She propped her chin in her hand. Could the same be said for her? West had kept a piece of himself hidden, hadn't wanted to reveal his real reasons for leaving Chicago. She'd done the same, though. She hadn't gone into any detail about her ex and didn't want to. Maybe it was best to keep things light for now, as they'd had so little of it since they'd met.

"So, let's show Monique and the rest of the bad guys that there's more to our relationship than hunting drones."

She skimmed her fork over the crumbs of tiramisu and licked it. "So, was this all a ruse?"

His gaze focused on her mouth, and then he swallowed. "Kind of. You can't allow thugs to dictate who you can and cannot see. You can't cower in your house until they decide you're no longer a target."

"I agree, or I never would've consented to this date."

He swept the napkin from his lap and crumpled it next to the empty dessert plate. "No running away from me in the street anymore?"

"Well, that depends." She laughed at his wide eyes.

"You, see? That's what I learned about you tonight." He wagged a finger at her. "You snort when you laugh."

West insisted on paying the bill and on following her home. When his car pulled in behind her truck, she pressed her hand against her belly and the butterflies raging inside.

Should she invite him in? Would he make a move? Should *she* make a move?

She stumbled from the truck and grabbed the door. Taking a deep breath, she made a decision and strode toward him.

He met her halfway and took her in his arms before she uttered one word. Wedging a knuckle beneath her chin, he tilted her head back and sealed his lips over hers. The taste of the tiramisu on his mouth made the kiss even sweeter.

If her knees felt weak before, they were positively jelly now. She sagged against him, wrapping her arms around his neck. How would they ever make it inside?

When they finally pulled apart, West said, "I'm sorry. I just couldn't wait any longer."

"Do you want to come inside?" She clawed inside her purse for her keys and found her phone buzzing instead. She fully intended to ignore the call until she saw it was Porter's phone.

"Sorry, this might be Olly or about Olly." She grabbed the phone and tapped it, her heart rate accelerating. "Hello?"

"Mom?"

She could barely make out Olly's whisper. "Speak up, Olly. I can't hear you. Is something wrong?"

Her son cleared his throat and continued in a louder stage whisper. "Mom, I buried it."

Blood pounded in her ears. "Buried what?"

"The memory card from the drone."

Chapter Fifteen

"What?!" Astrid's voice went up several octaves and even more decibels, as her face went completely white.

West's heart jumped to his throat. "What happened? Is Olly okay?"

She reached for his arm, and her fingernails dug into his skin. "Olly just told me he buried the drone's memory card."

Putting his hand on Astrid's stiff back, he nudged her toward the front door. "Let's get inside. Put the phone on speaker, so I can hear him."

Astrid put one foot in front of the other as she said, "Hold on a minute, Olly. Sheriff Chandler is with me. He wants to hear what you have to say."

Once on the porch, she spun around and yelped when Sherlock came up behind her and snuffled the back of her knees.

"It's okay. I have him." West hooked his fingers around the dog's collar and told him to stay.

Astrid's hands were shaking so badly, she couldn't put the key in the lock. West took the keys from her and unlocked the top and bottom. Sherlock trotted ahead of them and when West shut them all inside, Astrid rearmed the security system.

Carrying the phone in front of her as if it were a bomb,

she sat on the edge of the couch. She tapped the display and put the phone on the coffee table. "Okay, Olly. We're inside and I have the phone on speaker for Sheriff Chandler."

"Hey, Olly. Do you want to tell us what happened from the beginning? You're not in trouble. Nobody's in trouble." West took one of Astrid's fidgety hands in his own.

"I told you Logan and I took the drone, and some guy whacked it or something, so it was acting weird when we got it down. I tried to fix it, and that's when that little card fell out. I tried to put it back in, but that opening was bent or something. It wouldn't go back in, but I could jam the little door on the slot closed without the card in it. So, that's what I did. I put the card in my pocket."

Astrid darted a gaze at West and swept her tongue across her bottom lip. "Why didn't you just give it to me?"

"I forgot I had it until I was packing for the sleep-out. Then there was such a big deal about the drone, I was afraid to give it to you."

"That's what's been bothering you since you left?"

"Yeah, but since you told me Davia's buying another one, I figured I'd better tell you what happened." He paused, and it sounded like he gulped back some tears. "Sorry, Mom."

"Don't worry about it, Olly. I'm not happy with all this lying and secrecy, but you haven't done anything that can't be fixed." Astrid laced her fingers together and clamped her hands between her knees. "Why'd you bury the memory card?"

"Just didn't want anyone to catch me with it. You know how Mr. Monroe gets all nosy."

"Yeah, because that's his job. Nobody knows you have that card, or buried that card?"

"Only Logan, but he doesn't know where I buried it."

West hunched forward, elbows on his knees. "Where *did* you bury it, Olly?"

"I-I'm not really sure, Sheriff Chandler. Under some tree, down by the river where we were fishing."

West's eye twitched. Great. Possible evidence in a murder case buried in the mud somewhere.

He touched Astrid's arm as he spoke again. "Do you think you could show me, Olly?"

"Do you really want it that bad?" Olly whistled. "Do you think it might have who killed that guy on it?"

Astrid covered her mouth with her hand.

Stroking her arm, West answered Olly. "I don't really know, but I'd like to look at it, anyway."

Astrid blurted out. "Don't tell anyone about it, Olly. Y-you know, it could be a police thing, so just don't tell anyone, not even Mr. Monroe and not the other boys. Tell Logan to stay quiet, too. Just in case it messes up evidence."

"Yeah, sure." Olly blew out a long breath. "I'm glad I told you."

"Me, too. Enjoy yourself and don't think about it again. Sheriff Chandler will talk to Mr. Monroe about meeting you out there. He'll make up some reason."

"Oh." Olly sniffed. "You can't wait until camp is over in a few days?"

West said, "The memory card may already be corrupted, messed up. I just want to make sure it doesn't get any worse. It's all right, Olly. I'll talk to Mr. Monroe tomorrow morning about making my way out there. You can show me where it is then."

Astrid and Olly said their goodbyes, and Astrid ended the call. She sat still, staring at the phone in her hand. "All this time he had it. All this time he's been in danger."

"They don't know he has it. Why would they?" He rubbed a circle on her back. "I'll go out there tomorrow and hopefully Olly can tell me where he buried it. Once I have it, he…and you…will be safe—whether or not it contains the evidence we need."

Astrid growled and squeezed her hands together. "Ooh, I could strangle that kid. If he'd told me before he left and handed it over, none of this other stuff would've happened. Maybe even Naomi would be alive."

"Naomi's murder didn't have anything to do with the drone. The cartel must've believed that Naomi had information from Chase, information they couldn't afford getting out." The back rub turned to a caress of her shoulders. "Don't even think that. Olly did the right thing, and I'm going to take care of it tomorrow."

"I hope after all this, the footage actually proves useful."

"So do I." He pushed up from the couch, his hand still on her shoulder. "Go take a bubble bath, have a glass of wine, rub Sherlock's belly—whatever you need to do to relax. I'll get Monroe's phone number from you and call him tomorrow."

She grabbed his hand, her fingers threading through his. "Do you have to leave?"

A knot of desire formed in his belly. "I don't have to leave…if you don't want me to."

"You said whatever I need to do to relax." She stood up beside him and hooked her fingers in his belt loops. "I think I need you."

WHATEVER URGE CAME over him in the driveway when they got home seemed to claim him again, as he cupped the back of her head, sliding his fingers into her hair. She'd kicked off her heels when she sat on the couch to talk to Olly, so she and West no longer stood nose-to-nose. She compensated by rising on her tiptoes and pressing her mouth against his.

His lips parted, and she flicked the tip of her tongue inside his mouth as she pulled him closer. He groaned and deepened the kiss, moving his body against hers.

As Sherlock whined and thumped his tail against the floor, West whispered in her ear, "I don't need an audience."

She giggled but suppressed the snort this time. "You're right. It would probably traumatize him."

Taking West's hand, she took a step toward the stairs. Still connected, they walked up the staircase, West trailing behind her, the warmth emanating off his body.

When they got to her bedroom, West pulled his wallet and phone from his pocket and tossed them onto the nightstand. He removed his boots and socks, and started to unbutton his shirt while she watched him, her heart pounding.

"Let me." She shooed away his hands and took over the unbuttoning job. Her fingers were trembling so much, he probably could've made faster work of it, but she enjoyed savoring the anticipation.

When she had a few buttons left, West grabbed the hem of his shirt, plucked his T-shirt out of the waistband of his jeans and pulled the whole mess over his head. He let his clothes drop to the floor. "That's how it's done."

She smoothed her hands over his bare chest, the dark hair scattered there tickling her palms. "I like a man out of uniform almost as much as I like him in uniform."

"And here I thought you were giving up on cops." He traced his tongue along the lobe of her ear.

"Never say never." She tugged at his belt. "Do you have a shortcut for removing everything from the bottom half, as well?"

"Your turn." He fumbled with the small pearl buttons of her blouse until he had a couple open. Then he pinched the silky material between his fingers and lifted the blouse over her head.

She raised her arms to make it easy for him, and he twisted around to lay the blouse over the back of a chair. "It just looks so much nicer than my stuff, I didn't want to toss it on the floor."

"Should I be offended that you're thinking about the orderly disposal of my clothing and aren't lost in the moment, overcome with passion?"

Grabbing her wrist, he pressed her hand against the bulge in his jeans. "I'm so overcome with passion, I'm about to explode."

"Please don't." She cupped his crotch. "I have higher expectations than that."

"Don't worry. I plan to exceed every expectation you have." He flicked the bra straps from her shoulders and buried his face in the crook of her neck. "You smell like a fresh day in the forest in a field of wildflowers. Are there fields of wildflowers in the forest?"

"I'll show you sometime." She reached behind her and unclasped her bra. She let it fall to the floor and got goose bumps as West's gaze traced the curve of her breasts.

His hands replaced his gaze, and he skimmed his fingers along her skin, circling toward her nipples. Her breasts ached at his touch, and she arched her back for more contact.

He palmed her right breast, dipping his head to swirl his

tongue over her nipple. With her legs shaking, she wrapped an arm around his narrow waist and dug her nails into his back.

She gasped. "I can't do this standing up, Sheriff. If you're gonna take me, you'd better do it on the bed, horizontally."

"I can do horizontal." He took a step back from their heated contact and unbuckled his belt. Before she could add a helping hand, he'd peeled off his jeans and briefs, and they dropped to his knees...but her gaze landed north of his knees.

She circled her hand around his shaft and ran it up the length of him. He clenched his jaw and squeezed his eyes closed.

"I'm not doing this standing up, either." He wrapped both hands around her waist and swung her around to the bed where she landed with a plop. He kicked off the remainder of his clothing, and then he knelt before her and unzipped her black slacks.

As he tugged at the material, she lifted her hips. He pulled her slacks from her body and threw them over his shoulder. "Sorry, I don't give a damn about those pants right now."

"Right answer." Her words ended on a squeak as he parted her thighs with his rough palms and tickled her swollen folds with the tip of his tongue.

And she thought *he'd* have trouble holding himself together. The second his mouth touched her, her core tightened and every nerve ending throbbed in anticipation. Her fingers plowed through his hair, as she couldn't decide if she wanted him to stop or keep going forever.

Turned out forever meant minutes as her passion exploded, and a warm rush infused her senses. Like a hot river of lava, her release raced through her body, melting her previously tense muscles into sweet pudding.

She'd clasped her knees against West's head, and she didn't release him until her legs fell open in lethargic surrender. Running her finger down the bridge of her nose, she asked, "Did I cut off the circulation to your brain with my thighs?"

"If you did, I hardly noticed." He encircled her ankles with his long fingers and lifted her legs, resting her calves on his shoulders, damp with sweat. "That was a little fast. Are you ready for another?"

"We have all night, don't we?" She unwrapped her legs from his body and scooted back onto the bed, patting the mattress. "Join me."

Staying on his knees, he maneuvered to the nightstand and scooped up his wallet. He flipped it open and pulled out a foil packet of condoms. They unfurled as he jiggled them in the air. "I'm not saying I was hoping to get lucky tonight, but I did have some faith in the future—with you."

His words gave her pause and put the reins on her giddiness. The word *future* made her nervous. Could she have a future with this man or any other when the father of her son remained in witness protection, hiding from the people he double-crossed? If the future meant the next few hours, she could handle it.

"I-is this okay?" He cocked his head as his brows created a V over his nose.

"It's more than okay, Sheriff." She snatched the condoms from his fingers, detached the top packet and ripped it open with her teeth.

He entered her while pinning her with a gaze so full

of desire and hunger, she let go of every last reservation. She'd deal with the future…in the future.

THE FOLLOWING MORNING, Astrid woke up with West's arm heavy around her waist, his head on her pillow, his body crowding hers to the edge of the bed. She didn't even mind.

She inhaled the scent of him on her sheets, a little salty, a lot masculine, and stretched her legs, curling her toes in satisfaction. A passionate lover, West combined a tenderness with his fervent ardor, making her feel both desired and cherished.

She'd been in her early twenties when she'd married Russ and didn't know men could be sweet and fierce at the same time. She liked it.

Sherlock whined at the closed bedroom door, and she rolled off the mattress, landing on her bare feet. She'd assumed the dog was housebroken, but the poor thing had been cooped up for a while.

West stirred, and she tiptoed to the door and cracked it open. Sherlock's soft black nose snuffled into the space. Pushing the door wider, she said, "Sorry, boy. I'll let you out right now. Promise you won't run away—or drag anything home when you come back."

She yanked her terry-cloth robe from a hook on the back of the door and stuffed her arms in the sleeves. Belting the robe, she patted her thigh. "C'mon, Sherlock."

His nails clicked on the wood as he followed her downstairs. She sniffed the air and scanned the floor for any accidents. "You're a good boy, Sherlock."

She padded to the sliding door in the back and opened it enough to let Sherlock outside. With his tail waving, he scampered toward the tree line, and the forest sucked him into its interior.

Shoving her hands in her pockets, she watched until the shivering bushes where he disappeared stilled. She'd felt safe wrapped in West's arms last night. Maybe when he left, she'd have to invite Sherlock to hold vigil at the foot of her bed until West caught Chase's and Naomi's killer. He maybe could've done that a lot sooner if Olly hadn't kept that memory card a secret.

She couldn't help it. She studied Olly sometimes for signs that he shared his father's antisocial nature. He didn't. Her brother Tate had assured her that Olly's occasional lying and misbehavior did not veer from typical adolescent male conduct. Comparing notes with Sam, who'd helped raise her stepson Anton, and other boy moms, she tended to agree with Tate. At least Olly had come clean about everything.

"Is he coming back?"

Astrid whirled around, hand to her chest. "You scared me."

"Sorry." West held up his hands. "I thought you had regrets and were contemplating following Sherlock out to the woods until I left your house."

Her gaze flickered over his half-naked body, his tight briefs clinging to him in all the right places. She swallowed hard.

His stride ate up the space between them, and he slipped his hands inside her robe to shape her hips. "If you're gonna look at me like that, I might just have to carry you back upstairs."

Curling her arms around his neck, she stood on her tiptoes to reach his mouth with hers. She pressed her lips, still tender from their feverish kisses last night, against his.

She broke off the kiss and wedged her head beneath his chin. "I'd take you up on that, but you have something rather important to do today."

"That's why I came looking for you. Can you give me Porter Monroe's cell phone number, so I can let him know I'm coming out to the camp today?"

"My phone's charging on the kitchen counter." She pointed over his shoulder and disentangled herself from his arms. "I'll send you my contact info for Porter."

"Guess I'd better get my phone. I left it upstairs."

As he climbed the stairs, she watched the muscles of his backside bunch and release. Then she shook her head and called out. "And put some clothes on, will ya?"

She grabbed her phone and scrolled through her contacts. She tapped Porter's name to send it to West and checked her text messages. Her pulse quickened when she read one from Michelle Clark letting her know that she showed her husband the photos, and he was interested. This sale would be such a boost to her career—and she hadn't even needed the drone photos.

She texted Michelle back with some possible next steps, and then held her breath when she looked at her phone calls. No voice mails and nothing from any blocked numbers. Had Chase's drug contacts given up on her?

As long as they didn't know Olly was the one who had the memory card…if it was still any good. She wiped her sweaty palms against the terry cloth of her robe. The sexy interlude with West had wiped all the nagging thoughts from her mind, but it hadn't banished them completely.

West jogged down the stairs in bare feet, clutching his

phone, his jeans and T-shirt covering his assets—but now she knew what lurked beneath. He held up the phone. "Got it. Thanks. Coffee?"

"I can make some. Do you want some breakfast, too?" She set down her cell and turned to the cupboard for the coffee pods.

"Just some toast, if you have it. I can make it myself." He perched on a stool at the kitchen island and tapped his phone's display. He gave her a thumbs-up. "Porter Monroe? This is Sheriff Chandler."

West raised his eyebrows at Astrid and said, "No, not at all. You're not in any trouble. I need to drop by the camp today and speak with Olly Crockett. Can you make that happen?"

As Astrid put on the coffee, she kept one ear trained on West's conversation with Porter. She knew exactly why Porter thought the sheriff might be calling him with bad news.

West said, "I'll be sure to make it there by ten so that Olly can join the others for kayaking. Can you give me the directions? Yeah, yeah, that'll work."

When the call ended, West glanced at his phone. "He's texting the directions to me and to you, just in case I need a guide."

He pocketed the phone, and Astrid set a cup of coffee in front of him. "That Porter's a little paranoid, isn't he? I mean, I get why most people don't want to hear from law enforcement, but wow, he had his alibi all ready."

"Yeah, well, Porter has always enjoyed working with kids—even before he got married and had a daughter of his own. It led to a lot of suspicion around his activities. He was even questioned in the disappearance of some young boys."

He took a sip of his coffee, considering her words. "That explains his response. I should have you whispering in my ear all the time giving me the lowdown on all Dead Falls Island residents."

The lowdown on everyone but herself. He must already know about her ex's situation. She should at least explain to him how she wound up with a guy like Russ, but he owed her some truths, as well.

Cupping her mug, she stared into her coffee. "West, I know why you left Chicago and your department."

His hand jerked, and his coffee sloshed over the side. "I suppose everyone in town knows. It's easy to do a search. The incident was all over the news at the time."

"I didn't do the search. Somebody told me…but it's not like it's the talk of the town." She ran a thumb along the rim of her cup. "That must've been difficult for you."

A muscle twitched in the corner of his jaw. "It made me question everything. I wasn't sure I could continue in this career."

Touching his arm, she said, "The boy was pointing a gun at you. He'd shot a child before. You had no reason to think his gun wasn't loaded and that he'd shoot you, too."

"I know all of that." He clasped the back of his neck. "It didn't help much at the time."

"But now? Have you come to terms with it now?" She grabbed the coffee pot to get him a refill and get out of his space.

Before he could answer her, his phone rang, and he spun it around to face him. "Porter calling. Maybe he wants me there earlier."

He tapped his display twice. "Porter, I have you on speaker phone, and Olly's mom is with me. Change of time?"

"Oh, h-hello, Astrid. I'm afraid there's a problem, Sheriff."

Astrid put down the coffee pot, her hands suddenly unsteady. "What's the problem, Porter?"

"We can't find Olly."

Chapter Sixteen

"Can't find him?" Astrid gripped the edge of the counter, her mouth suddenly dry. "What does that mean, Porter? Did he go somewhere and not return, yet?"

"Not exactly like that, Astrid." Porter took a deep breath. "The boys get up at seven to wash up and start preparing breakfast. We do a head count when they're in the mess area of the campsite. We did the head count and came up short. When we asked if any of the boys noticed anyone missing, Logan Davidson said Olly wasn't in their tent this morning. He figured he'd gone into the bushes to take care of business."

West picked up the phone, speaking into it. "How long had Olly been gone between the time Logan woke up and when you asked at breakfast?"

Astrid chewed on her bottom lip, the coffee taste in her mouth rancid. She closed her eyes and took a deep breath. Olly just wandered off. He did that sometimes.

Porter responded, "Logan woke up a little before the seven a.m. camp-wide alarm. He washed, dressed and was in the mess area by seven fifteen. They all have to be there by that time."

"So, we're talking about twenty to thirty minutes?" West scratched at the stubble on his jaw.

"That's right." Porter coughed. "Before you ask, all of us Scout leaders were in our area of the camp. Nobody arose before our own alarm at six forty-five. A few of the teen camp counselors have already gone out looking for him. Olly does like to fish, and he kept telling us about a fishing spot he wanted to try. One of the teenage boys went down there."

"I'm going to head out there myself, Porter. Keep looking. I'll send in a few more deputies if he hasn't turned up by the time I get there. Keep me posted."

"You got it, Sheriff. A-and, Astrid. I'm sure there's nothing to worry about. Olly has a good sense of direction and a good set of skills. There must be some reason he went off on his own. Like I said before, he'd been a little out of sorts when he got here, but he was getting back on track. Maybe he wanted to make up for some lost time or something. I'm sure we'll find him."

Astrid cleared her throat in an effort to command her voice before answering. "Thanks, Porter."

When the call ended, West squeezed her shoulder. "Don't worry. I'll find him."

She knotted her fingers in front of her. "Do you think he went off in search of the memory card himself? Maybe he felt guilty about not telling me and burying it, so he figured he'd find it for you before you came."

"He could've done that. Porter didn't mention that Logan had said anything about the card." West tossed back another gulp of coffee and put his cup in the sink. "I'll talk to Logan when I get there. Maybe Olly told his friend more about that card than he let on to us. Maybe Logan knows exactly where Olly is and is keeping mum out of a sense of loyalty."

"When *you* get there?" Her cup clattered in the sink as it joined his. "When *we* get there. I can't sit around here all morning waiting for your phone call."

"Okay. You might have a better idea of where he might've gone, anyway, or Logan might feel more comfortable talking to you. I'll call out more deputies if Olly hasn't turned up in a few hours. He knows how to swim, right? He's been fishing in rivers and knows about currents?"

"He knows all that stuff, but he also knows not to go wandering off without telling an adult." Astrid folded her arms, digging her fingers into her biceps and dropping her gaze to the floor.

"What is it?"

"Last year, someone lured Olly out of his bed in the middle of the night by pretending to be his father. Olly didn't tell me about it. Just sneaked out of the house."

"He knows his father…isn't available right now, doesn't he? There's no way his father would be contacting him now."

So, Sam hadn't been the only one conducting searches. Astrid nodded, tears pricking the back of her eyeballs. "He knows, but…"

"But what?"

"But what if someone else lured him away?" She hunched her shoulders to her ears, every muscle in her body taut and aching. "What if the drug dealers know he has the memory card?"

"How could they? We didn't even know until last night when he called." West's voice sounded firm, but a muscle twitched in the corner of his clenched jaw, and he wouldn't meet her gaze.

The same scenario must've occurred to him, which

made it even more real to Astrid. Despite her seized-up muscles, her teeth began to chatter.

West folded her in his arms and stroked her hair. "That prospect seems unlikely. They don't know he has the memory card. Even if they suspect it, they don't know where he is or how to get there. The camp seems remote to me. Porter told me I'd never find it on my GPS. That's why he gave me detailed directions."

She pressed her nose against the front of his shirt and sniffled. "They just seem to know everything."

"We'll find him, Astrid. Maybe he'll return before we even get to the camp. He's a smart, resourceful boy." He pulled her away from his chest and winked. "Look how long he kept you in the dark about his antics with the drone."

She gave him a shaky laugh. "I'm going to take a quick shower and get dressed. You can use the bathroom off Tate's room."

She took the stairs two at a time to avoid breaking down in front of him. How could it be a coincidence that he went missing the morning after he told her about burying the memory card? Unless he really did go off on his own to find it before West got there. That's something Olly would do. He always tried to make things right. He'd always tried to fix things for her when she and Russ would fight, or rather when Russ would rage at her for no reason. It broke her heart. A child shouldn't have to fix anything for his parents.

When she reached the bathroom, she let the robe drop at her feet. She stepped in the shower and cranked on the hot water, allowing it to stream down her back in an attempt to wash away her guilt. She'd been frolicking in bed with West when her little boy needed her.

She showered quickly and poked her head out of the bathroom door. When she heard the water running from Tate's bathroom, she wrapped the robe around her and scurried across the hall to her bedroom.

Her gaze darted across the room. All evidence of her passionate night with West had disappeared. He'd even neatly draped her slacks over the back of the chair and picked up her underwear. The bed might be a little more tousled than usual—along with her feelings—but she'd have to put last night behind her...for now.

She pulled on a pair of jeans and a long-sleeved T-shirt and dug her hiking boots out of the closet. She was prepared to walk miles to find Olly.

Gray skies met her when she pulled open her blinds, so she yanked a flannel shirt from a hanger to wear beneath her jacket. In the shade of the forest, especially around the bodies of water, the air could turn chilly.

She scooped her hair into a ponytail and jogged downstairs. As she grabbed her jacket from the coat closet in the foyer, West clumped down the stairs in the clothes he wore yesterday.

Tilting her head, she said, "You might need a jacket."

"I have one in my car. We'll ride over together. I figure having a local with me will get us there faster."

"Any more calls from Porter...or anyone else?" She veered around him to grab Sherlock's bowl from the counter. She dumped three cups of dry kibble into his dish. "I'd better leave this on the porch for Sherlock."

"Haven't heard from Porter. I gave my desk sergeant a heads-up about the situation, though. He told me it's common for kids to take off or get lost in the woods, even during the organized camps."

"I know that." She disarmed the security system and swung open the door with a whistle on her lips. "But we both know this is not an ordinary circumstance for an ordinary boy."

"Then we'd better get going." West squared his jaw as he met her on the porch.

Sherlock hadn't responded to her whistle, so she set the dish down on the porch. Her gaze tracked along the tree line. "I hope he returns."

She meant Sherlock, but she was thinking about Olly.

WEST'S GUT CHURNED with anxiety as he drove toward the Scout camp in the forest, following Astrid's directions. He'd tried to keep a positive outlook for Astrid's sake, but Olly's disappearance on the heels of his information last night didn't bode well for the boy.

If anything happened to Astrid's son on his watch, that dark vortex of guilt would pull him back, erasing all the progress he'd made over the past several months. But was it really progress or just stuffing down and ignoring his feelings?

His lips twisted. He'd been to so many therapy sessions, he couldn't imagine what feeling he'd ignored. Dr. Charmaine had forced him to lay bare everything and examine it in the harsh light of truth. He didn't have one feeling left he hadn't analyzed and probed.

At least Astrid hadn't turned away from him in disgust when she confronted him about his past.

She tapped him on the thigh, bringing him out of his reverie. "Right, right, right after the bend. Pay attention, Sheriff, or you'll get us lost, too."

West sucked in a breath. "Do you think Olly is lost?"

"He could be." She pressed her hands against her bouncing knees. "I mean, maybe he started out looking for the spot where he buried the memory card. Then he took a few wrong turns and got lost. He did tell us last night he probably could tell you where he buried it. He didn't sound absolutely sure about the location. There are a lot of trees out there, and most of them look the same."

"That's possible." West kept his tone light and tried not to strangle the steering wheel, but Astrid shot him a side glance. He tried on a smile, which seemed to make things worse as her knees started bouncing again.

After their last turnoff, they reached a trailhead, and West recognized the crossed branches of a red alder that Porter had described to him as being the starting off point to the scout camp.

He'd given silent thanks to the previous sheriff for the tip about keeping hiking boots in both his personal car and DFSD vehicle. The street boots he'd worn to dinner last night wouldn't cut it in these woods. Next purchase should be a four-wheel drive vehicle for his personal use.

Twisting around, he reached into the back seat. "Sheriff Hopkins warned me about keeping appropriate footwear with me at all times on the island."

"How about that?" Astrid lifted her eyebrows at the pair of boots in his hand. "Sheriff Hopkins was good for something, after all."

West cracked open his door and swapped his shoes while Astrid wandered to his side of the car. As he tied the boots, he said, "You're all kind of rough on Hopkins. Was he really that bad?"

"Just not dedicated. Kind of lazy. Didn't want to go out

of his way." She shrugged and rubbed her hands together, her focus on the trail.

"Seems he knew what he was *supposed* to be doing because he gave me some good advice." He stomped his boots on the mushy ground. "A lot of cops think they can take a top job in a small town and ease into retirement."

"Is that what you figured?"

"I'd done my research. I knew Dead Falls Island offered a prime spot for drug trafficking between the US and Canada…and I'm not ready to retire yet." He slammed the car door. "Let's go find Olly."

They tromped up the trail and Astrid confirmed his suspicions. She was an outdoor girl through and through. She could probably survive in the wilderness on her own for days—he hoped her son followed in Mom's footsteps.

Fifteen minutes of uphill later, a scattering of army green tents appeared through the trees. Astrid strode into the campsite looking better than when they started, and he brought up the rear only slightly out of breath. A gym in the city didn't quite prepare you for this kind of exertion.

On the lookout for them, Porter rushed forward. "The teen Scouts haven't found anything yet."

Astrid did the introductions. "Porter Monroe, this is Sheriff West Chandler. Have you met yet?"

"Not yet." Porter grabbed West's hand in a firm grip. "Good to meet you, Sheriff. Sorry it's under these circumstances. This has never happened before on one of my trips."

"I'm sure Astrid doesn't blame you, Porter. Thanks for calling so quickly and taking decisive actions."

Astrid said, "Not at all, Porter."

West turned his head to watch the boys stuffing their

backpacks as they roughhoused, oblivious to the seriousness of their missing friend.

Porter jerked his thumb at them. "We figured we'd go ahead with our regular activities. We don't want to spook the boys."

"I agree, but we'd like to talk to Olly's friend Logan."

"I have him waiting for you in the counselors' tent." Porter gestured for them to follow him. "He hasn't said much since we questioned him earlier."

Drawing up beside Porter, Astrid asked, "Did Logan seem scared or worried about Olly?"

"Nope, but Sheriff Chandler can determine that for himself." Porter whipped aside the flap of a large canvas tent, and a boy with curly dark hair jerked his head up.

"Hi, Ms. Mitchell. Am I in trouble?" Logan's big brown eyes darted toward West.

"Hi, Logan. You're not in any trouble. Are you having fun at camp?" Astrid sat next to him on a camp chair.

"Yeah, sort of. Olly and I caught the biggest fishes yesterday."

"Did you eat them? Were they any good?" West dragged a chair over and sat across from Astrid and Logan.

"Umm, yeah, they were okay. I don't really like fish." Logan scrunched up his freckled nose.

Rolling his shoulders, West leaned back in the small chair. He shifted his jaw back and forth, trying to loosen the tension. If he came off as too intense, the kid wouldn't open up to him—and he always tensed up around kids.

"Olly's your best friend, right?"

"Yeah." Logan's gaze shifted to Astrid, and she gave him an encouraging smile.

West wanted to ease into the interrogation, but they didn't

have time to waste. "When was the last time you saw Olly, Logan?"

"At lights-out." Logan rubbed his nose with the back of his hand. "We were in our sleeping bags in our tent. We were talking, and then fell asleep. Tyler and Colt were in there, too."

Astrid asked, "Were you and Olly talking to Tyler and Colt?"

"Naw. They fell asleep before us."

"After you fell asleep, you didn't see Olly again?" West uncrossed his arms, letting them fall loosely in his lap.

"Nope." Logan cranked his head back and forth like a robot.

"Did you hear him get up at night or in the morning?" Astrid scooted a little closer to Logan and brushed his arm with her knuckles.

"Nooo." Logan drew out the word, and his face paled, making his freckles pop.

West didn't have kids, but he knew a liar when he saw and heard one. Spreading his hands, West said, "It's okay if you did hear something and didn't say anything to Mr. Monroe. Maybe you forgot. Did you forget, Logan?"

"Uh-uh." He shook his head hard this time and had to brush his floppy brown hair from his eyes.

"Logan." Astrid turned her body so that her knees bumped the boy's. "What did you and Olly talk about last night?"

Logan's brown eyes widened, looking like two saucers in his sharp face. "Nothing. Fishing."

Astrid squeezed Logan's knee. "It's okay to tell us, Logan. Olly already informed us that he mentioned the drone's memory card to you."

"That's right, Logan." West shrugged. "So we know all about that, and Olly's not in any trouble over it. I just figured that's what you two were talking about before you went to sleep. Right?"

"Yeah." Logan nibbled on a raggedy nail.

West eased out a long breath. "Okay, yeah. Olly told us he buried it but couldn't exactly remember where. Is that what he told you?"

"Uh-huh." Logan sat forward in his seat. "We were going to go hunting for it today if we could sneak away after the kayaking."

Astrid's smile tightened on her face, and she shoved an unsteady hand through her hair. "Do you think he went by himself to find it before breakfast?"

Logan dipped his head and swung one leg back and forth, the heel of his sneaker hitting the chair on the backswing. "N-no."

"Why do you say that?" A muscle at the corner of West's eye danced out of control, and he wanted to slap it into submission before it terrified Logan.

"He might've gone looking for it, but he didn't go alone." Logan twisted his head toward Astrid. "Am I gonna get in trouble?"

"Not at all, Logan." Astrid tucked her hands beneath her thighs. "What do you mean, he didn't go alone?"

Deciding on the truth, Logan straightened up in his chair and planted both feet on the ground. "I mean, I heard Olly leave last night...but he wasn't by himself. Some woman woke him up and took him away."

Chapter Seventeen

Astrid's blood felt ice cold running through her veins, and her head swam as she opened and closed her mouth like one of those fish the boys caught yesterday.

Luckily, Logan had locked onto West, probably trying to judge the sheriff's reaction.

West's twitching eye and tight jaw confirmed Astrid's thudding dread. He knew what she suspected. Chase's killers had somehow found out Olly had the drone's memory card and…what? What did they have planned for him? What if he couldn't lead them to the card?

When the silence seemed to have stretched on for an eternity, West cleared his throat. "Someone woke up Olly to help him find the memory card?"

"I guess." Logan licked his lips. "I didn't wanna say anything because I didn't wanna get Olly in trouble. He told me not to say anything to anyone about the drone thing. I thought maybe he called this woman to help him or something."

"Maybe he did." West ran a hand over his mouth and down the dark stubble on his chin. "Did you see the woman, Logan?"

"I pretended I was asleep because I didn't want to go with them. It's too cold at night."

"I agree. Good move." West gave Logan a thumbs-up. "Did you hear her voice?"

Logan lifted his shoulders to his ears. "They were whispering, but I could tell it was a girl."

Astrid couldn't take it anymore. She jumped up from the chair, knocking it over and making Logan jerk in his seat like a puppet. Wringing her hands in front of her, she asked, "Why'd Olly go with her, Logan? Why'd he just get up out of his sleeping bag and leave the tent in the middle of the night?"

Wrong move. Logan's skinny body stiffened, and he whipped his head toward the entrance to the tent, looking ready to bolt.

Astrid smoothed her hands against the thighs of her jeans. "I-I mean, did it seem like he knew her? I guess that's why he'd go with her, right, Sheriff Chandler?"

"Maybe. Better pick up that chair, or Mr. Monroe's gonna think we messed up the tent." West winked at Logan.

"Oh, we don't want that." Astrid smiled stiffly at Logan.

West gave her a little nod. "Can we get back to the woman's voice, Logan? You knew she was a female. Did you notice anything else about it?"

Logan squeezed his eyes closed and puffed out his cheeks. Astrid could kiss him for his level of concentration.

A breath hissed out of his puckered lips. "Yeah, she called him a funny name. I mean, she called him Olly, too, so I know she knew him, but she called him another name."

Astrid had taken her seat next to Logan again and gulped before asking. "What other name?"

Logan rolled his eyes upward and pressed his lips together. "Moshare."

"Moshare?" Astrid frowned. She'd been fearful of Logan's answer, but this didn't make sense.

West shifted in his too-small chair. "Moshare. Did she say it like this, Logan? *Mon cher*?"

West's French accent had Astrid curling her fingers around the arm of her jacket and holding her breath. West had told her yesterday that Chase's girlfriend was French, and her anonymous caller had pronounced Astrid's own name with a slight accent.

Logan screwed up one side of his face. "Yeah, I guess so."

"One more question, and then we'll let you join the others." West held up one finger. "What time did this woman come into the tent?"

Logan glanced longingly at the tent opening. "I dunno. It was dark. We can't have our phones, but I fell back asleep after they left."

"D-did Olly seem scared?" Astrid clenched her teeth and buried her fists in her lap.

"Olly scared?" Logan's eyes bugged out. "Naw. Olly's never scared, Ms. Mitchell."

West thrust out his hand to Logan. "Thanks, Logan. You did a good job."

Logan's cheeks flushed as he shook West's hand. Then he turned to Astrid. "When Olly comes back, tell him to come find me."

"I'll do that." Astrid gave him a misty smile and swiped her fingers beneath her nose.

As Logan hopped up, West put a finger to his lips. "Let's just keep this between us right now. We don't want everyone out there looking for the memory card, right?"

"I can keep a secret." Logan drew a cross on his chest.

She waited until Logan went outside the tent, and then covered her face with her hands, letting out a low moan. "They have him, don't they? Those drug dealers found out Olly had the memory card, and they took him."

West perched on the edge of the chair Logan just vacated, bumping his knees against hers. "They just want that card. They're not going to hurt him."

Lifting her head, she swiped a tear from her cheek. "What if he can't give them the card? What if he can't remember where he buried it? They didn't believe me when I told them I didn't have it."

"He's a kid. They'll figure he'll give it up if he knows where it is." West scratched his scruff, and the tic that had been fluttering at the corner of his eye moved to his jaw.

"What?" She dug her fingers into his thigh. "What are you thinking?"

"I'm just wondering how they discovered Olly had the card and how they found this campsite. You don't think…"

"I'm not thinking anything right now, and you're driving me further into a panic. Just spit it out."

"Maybe someone bugged your house when they broke in. How else did they find out? You didn't know Olly had that memory card until he called last night and told you."

Astrid gasped and gripped the seat of her chair. "Bugged my house? That's terrifying."

"I don't know. Would they have been that desperate that early?"

She replied, "That wouldn't explain it, anyway. We may have talked about Olly in the house having that card, but we didn't read out those directions that Porter texted to us."

Hearing his name, Porter poked his head in the tent. "Was Logan any help?"

Astrid glanced at West. Would he tell Porter that Olly had been kidnapped from his tent? Porter would panic and probably cause all the boys and their parents to panic, too, even though the kidnapper posed no danger to the other boys.

West pushed to his feet. "Not really. He and Olly talked in the tent before they fell asleep and when Logan woke up, Olly was gone. I am going to start a search though, and I'm calling in a few deputies. Obviously, stay alert for any signs of Olly."

"I'm so sorry, Astrid." Porter lifted his hat and ran a hand over his head. "I don't know why Olly would go off like that. Do you suspect any foul play, Sheriff?"

"Too soon to tell, Porter. You can tell the boys Olly wandered off, but just carry on."

"Okay. Anything more we can do, Sheriff, let us know."

Astrid cocked her head. "You told Logan to keep quiet, and you skirted the truth with Porter. What's your reasoning?"

"If Olly is tramping around the forest with this French woman, I don't want her spooked. I don't want to alert her that we're onto them. We'll search first, and I'll have a few of the deputies canvass the area." He snapped his fingers. "I do need more info from Porter, though. If Olly buried the card when he was on a Scout excursion, we need to know where they went yesterday so we can search that area."

"You should probably catch him before the boys head out." Astrid massaged her temples, as all the tension of the morning pounded in her head. "While you're talking to Porter, I can check the tent and Olly's sleeping bag. Maybe he left some kind of clue there."

"Porter already checked the tent, but definitely have a look."

"Don't leave without me. I'm going to search for Olly, too." Astrid straightened her spine. "I have a feeling Olly isn't just going to lead this woman to the card. He knows how important it is to your case. Maybe he'll stall her. He knows this forest well."

West clasped the back of his neck, a frown creasing his brow. "Hang on. You were making a point when Porter came in and interrupted us. You said, and I agree, that Monique and her cohorts couldn't have found out the location of the campsite from bugging your house because we didn't discuss those directions."

"That's right, unless they found out another way. I suppose they could've asked around town. You said that Monique was hanging around Dead Falls with Chase."

"Yeah, but where did we discuss both the fact that Olly had the memory card and buried it and the location of the campsite?"

Astrid swallowed. "My phone."

"Yeah."

"Y-you think my phone's bugged?" She pawed through her purse to find her cell and cupped it in her hand, eyeing it as if it was getting ready to bite her.

"It could be."

"How? Someone was able to do that remotely?" She tapped her phone to access it, clicking through the apps as if one of them could tell her someone was listening to her calls and reading her texts.

"That would take a high level of technical expertise to do it remotely, but…"

"You mean someone did it physically? How could that happen without my knowledge?"

West shrugged. "People leave their phones unattended all the time. One of my deputies informed me this week, it doesn't take long to bypass someone's security code on the phone if you know what you're doing."

She held her phone out to him. "Do you know what you're doing?"

"No, but my deputy Amanda does." He plucked it from her hand. "We can have her take a look, but can you think of any time this week when you left your phone?"

"A few times, but I don't believe some stranger could've picked up my phone, broken into it and bugged it."

"Think." He tapped his head. "Maybe it wasn't a stranger."

She blinked. "One of my friends? A coworker? No way."

When West's phone rang, Astrid started, her frayed nerves playing havoc with her reflexes. They needed to get out there now and start looking for Olly and this woman.

She pinned West with an expectant gaze when he answered his phone. Could this be some news already?

Maybe he felt the heat of her stare because he put the phone on speaker as he picked up the call. "Sheriff Chandler."

A low, rough voice rasped over the line. "Sheriff, this is Jackson Cross, the bartender at the Crab."

"Yeah, I remember. What can I do for you?"

Astrid tapped her foot. If this was some barroom brawl, she hoped West could send one of his deputies.

"Oh, me? I'm all good, but I have some information you might be interested in."

"Go on."

"That French broad Monique you were looking for?"

"Yeah?" West glanced at her, and she crossed her arms, holding on tight.

"She's here at the Salty Crab. Came in about ten minutes ago, looked around, took a seat by the window. Ordered a Bloody Mary and looks like she's waiting on someone."

"You're sure?"

"Absolutely." Jackson hacked. "That fool Benji's in here already drooling over his first beer of the day. Her appearance surprised the hell out of me, too. Told you she didn't come in here. Thought you might want to know."

"Thanks, Jackson. I'm coming right over. Call me if it looks like she's leaving."

"Will do, boss."

When West ended the call, he pocketed his phone and said, "We found Monique."

Astrid ran her tongue across her teeth, her mouth suddenly parched. "That's great but if Monique is in the Salty Crab, who the hell has Olly?"

Chapter Eighteen

"That's what we're going to find out." West took Astrid by the shoulders, his tone unwavering. He didn't know if he was trying to convince her or himself. He had to save this boy.

"You mean you're going to the Salty Crab right now? Now, while Olly is out there somewhere with God knows who?" She wrenched away from him and grabbed her purse. "I'm going to find him. This is more than a case to me. He's my boy. He's my world. I don't expect you to get it. He's not *your* child."

He staggered back. Her words lashed him, flaying his skin raw, peeling it back and leaving him exposed. He'd heard these cries before from another mother. There was nothing he could do about that mother's pain, but he'd fix this. He'd make it right.

He squeezed his eyes closed for a brief moment, and then scooped in a deep breath. "It's not logical for me to go thrashing through the woods looking for Olly, who's no longer with his abductor. Do you think they're on the trails, sharing water and gushing over the flora and fauna together? They're not going to be in the open, waiting for someone to find them. Olly's abductor will be hiding with him, staying off the main trails. Keeping quiet when they hear voices. Maybe even ready to take drastic measures when confronted."

Astrid's anger seemed to seep from her body, and her shoulders rolled forward. "I-I'm sorry. What do you have in mind?"

"You don't have to apologize to me. I get it. I know your impulse is to charge out there, shouting his name." He put a hand over his hammering heart. "It's mine, too, but Jackson gave us an opportunity. Monique is the one who lured Olly from the tent. She either knows where he is or knows who has him. I'd say she's a good starting point for narrowing down our search."

Astrid gave him a jerky nod. "I understand. But I'm coming with you. Maybe Monique is a mother. Maybe she'll listen to me."

West didn't want Astrid anywhere near Monique, but he didn't want to tell her that yet. He could take her along to the Crab and maybe send her off on another errand while he talked to Monique, as he doubted the woman would be susceptible to a mother's pleas.

"Okay, let's go."

On the way out of the campsite, West stopped to speak to the Scout leader left behind to find out where the group had gone the day before. The man also told him the teens were still canvassing the area, looking for Olly.

As West hiked back to his vehicle, he prayed that the young men wouldn't stumble across something they couldn't handle…and then he said the same prayer for himself.

THEY DROVE INTO TOWN, Astrid fidgeting beside him the entire journey. He reached over and put his hand over both of hers, entwined in her lap. "Let's take this slow and easy.

We can't go rushing in there accusing Monique of taking Olly and demanding his location. I don't even want her to know that we know."

"Okay, okay." Her lip quivered, but otherwise she looked ready to do battle.

He parked his car one block over from the Crab and called Jackson at the bar. "Is she still there?"

"Still here. On her second Bloody Mary, and her friend joined her. Man, we haven't had class like these two in this bar since the ribbon-cutting ceremony."

"Man in a suit?" Had the big bosses come out for a little kid and a drone?

"No, no, a woman. Black hair, like Monique's, dressed up in some expensive threads, high heels, long talons for fingernails, big gobs of jewelry, the whole nine yards."

"I'm on my way in shortly. Don't make a big deal out of seeing me there."

"C'mon, Sheriff. You know we don't like the law at the Salty Crab."

As West ended the call, Astrid grabbed his arm. "Oh my God. I think I know Monique's companion."

"What? You know the woman who's with Monique?"

"That description matches a client of mine, Michelle Clark." Astrid's grip tightened. "And she had access to my phone."

"When was this?"

"A few days ago." She released his arm and clamped a hand over her mouth. "It was when we found the blank memory card on the ground at the Misty Hollow property. Michelle probably put it there."

West's gaze tracked to the corner. He didn't want to

let either one of those women in the Crab out of his sight. "And the phone?"

"I'd left it in the car. She told me the battery on her own had died, and she wanted to continue taking pictures of the property to send to her husband. She insisted on going back to the car to get the phone." Astrid smacked her hand on the dash. "She must've done it then."

"Tell me everything you know about Michelle Clark."

When Astrid had finished telling him what little info she had on her client, he called the station to relay the information to Deputy Fletcher. "If Amanda's there, have her do a deep search on this woman."

Astrid turned to him, her hands excitedly flapping around her. "This is perfect, West. I pretend I don't know anything about either one of them or the phone. Seeing Michelle with Monique will give me an excuse to talk to both women."

"Then what?" West squeezed the back of his neck. He didn't like the idea of Astrid talking to those women. They were capable of anything.

"Then… I don't know. Maybe I can get information out of them. Maybe I can at least let them know that nobody is onto them."

Closing his eyes, West dug his fingers into his temples. "I have an idea."

ASTRID TOOK SEVERAL steadying breaths as she strode toward the Salty Crab. Before reaching the door, she adjusted the wire West had taped to her chest.

She jerked open the door and made a beeline for the bar, not looking at the smattering of customers in for a prelunch drink. She leaned on the bar and waved to the bartender, a man she'd seen in passing a few times around town.

"Hey, Jackson. Can you do me a Bloody Mary?"

"Absolutely, Astrid." He cocked his head. "A little early for you, isn't it?"

She let out a sigh. "Yeah, apparently my son decided to sneak out of his tent last night on the Scout trip. It's not the first time he's pulled a stunt like this, but it had better be his last."

"Sorry to hear that, Astrid. Sounds like you need that drink." Jackson winked at her.

Astrid glanced to her right, her gaze sweeping across the two women sitting at the window, their heads together in furious, whispered conversation. She felt like grabbing Monique by the hair and demanding answers. Instead, she did a double-take and widened her eyes. "Michelle? Just the person I need to see."

"Oh, hello, Astrid. I was going to call you today." Michelle scooted away from the table and the younger woman across from her.

Astrid had to pounce before Monique left. As Jackson put the drink in front of her, Astrid nodded her thanks and carried the glass to the table with the two women. She dragged a chair over from the next table.

"Did your husband have a chance to look at all the pictures?"

"He did." Michelle puckered her lips in a pout. "I'm still working on him."

Astrid deliberately shifted her eyes to Monique, sucking down the last of her Bloody Mary. She smiled and raised her eyebrows.

Michelle tapped her fingernails on the table. "This is Monique. She's staying at the Bay View, and we met over breakfast. I'm sorry, sweetie, I didn't catch your last name."

"Monique Girard." She held out her hand for a limp shake.

"If you're looking for property on the island, let me know." Astrid slid her card toward Monique, noting a long scratch on the young woman's face. Astrid tapped her own cheek. "Ouch. Cat get you?"

Monique shrugged. "I was on a hike earlier and a tree branch smacked me in the face. Should've been paying attention."

"Obviously." Michelle's red lips tightened, and then she stirred her drink, the ice clinking against the side of the glass. "Did I hear you mention something about your son, Astrid?"

That reminded Astrid that she'd better take a sip, even though she hated Bloody Marys. She stuck the straw in her mouth, and the tangy concoction hit the back of her throat. "Yeah, I got a call from the camp this morning that he'd sneaked out of his tent."

"Oh, no." Michelle clicked her tongue. "You must be worried."

"I am, but it's not like he hasn't done this before. He's made a habit of it, so I'm sure he's just trying to make life difficult for the Scout leaders. He knows the woods very well, so I'm not afraid that he's in danger from the elements." She lifted her drink. "I just need a break before I start looking for him. My nerves are frazzled."

"I'm sure they are. You have my sympathies." Michelle flicked her fingers. "I have a daughter myself who was always wayward, and I told you my son has issues. What are you going to do?"

Her color high, Monique shoved back her chair. "I have to leave now. Thank you for the drink, Michelle. Nice to meet you, Astrid."

"*Drinks*, sweetie." Michelle tapped Monique's empty glass. "You had two of those."

Monique laughed. "You're right. I'll owe you if I see you before you check out."

When Monique left, Michelle turned back to Astrid. "My husband had some additional questions. Do you have a minute now?"

"Of course." Astrid sat through Michelle's fake questions, knowing the other woman couldn't care less about the answers.

When Michelle's phone buzzed, she glanced at it. "Oh, I have to leave. I'll be in touch before I leave the island."

"I hope so."

Michelle settled her tab with Jackson and even paid for Astrid's drink, which was nice of her considering she'd kidnapped her son.

When the door shut behind Michelle, Astrid dipped her head. "Hope that was okay."

She didn't expect an answer from West, sitting in his car, as this was a one-way bug, so she pushed back from the table and approached the bar. "Thanks for playing along, Jackson. You've been a big help."

"I just hope the sheriff tells me what this was all about when it's over."

"I'm sure you'll hear about it. I'm sure everyone will hear about it." She exchanged her Bloody Mary for a Diet Coke and as she turned back to the window table Jackson snapped his fingers.

"When you walked in, you could see the two of them going at it."

"Yeah, they didn't look too happy." She cocked her head. "Could you hear what they were arguing about?"

He rubbed a spot on the bar with a cloth. "They were whispering or talking low, but every once in a while, the younger one would get excited and raise her voice. I heard her say something about how it wasn't her fault she lost something. Then the older woman would shush her."

"Lost something? Yeah, I guess that makes sense." Astrid returned to the table, waiting for the next step in the plan.

She didn't have to wait long for her phone to start buzzing. She answered it just as if she would if no one was listening in. "Hi, West. Any luck?"

"Sorry, Astrid. The teenage Scouts haven't found him yet."

She closed her eyes and moderated her tone. "I know he's done this before, but I just can't help thinking he went off to find the buried drone card so that he could give it to you to make up for keeping it. If he couldn't remember where he left it, he might be looking for it now. O-or he could've gotten hurt and can't make his way back."

The little sob at the end was for real.

"You said he knows the forest. Where would he go if he couldn't find his way back to the camp?"

"He'd go to the falls, West. All the kids know how to get to the falls. Hell, maybe he even put the memory card there and didn't want to tell me because he's not supposed to go to the falls by himself. It's about three miles from the camp, but that's nothing to Olly." She held her breath, waiting for West's response, the response that would hopefully lure Olly's captors to a specific location—as long as her son was still leading them on a wild goose chase out there.

"In the caves? Do you think he's in those caves behind the falls?"

She drew in a breath. "Yes. That would make total sense.

He told me he couldn't remember where he buried the card because he didn't want to admit he'd been to those caves. He didn't want to tell you, either, when you arrived, so he figured he'd get the card himself. That has to be it, West. He has to be at those caves. Maybe he got stuck and can't make his way out."

"Then that's where we'll start looking. Where are you? I'll pick you up."

"I'm at the Salty Crab. I'm sorry, but I needed a drink."

"Totally understandable. I'll swing by and pick you up."

"Hurry, West. I'm starting to get worried."

When they ended the call, Astrid slipped her phone into her purse, feeling as if she had ticking time bomb in there. Would Michelle and Monique take the bait and send their goons to the falls with Olly? What would Olly make of it? If he'd left the card somewhere else, he'd be happy to go along with them to lead them astray.

But what if that's exactly where he *did* leave the card? Would he try to dissuade them from heading to the falls? Would he be able to bluff them? Would they hurt him if they figured that out? He was just a kid.

She pushed away from the table and waved to Jackson on her way out the door. "Thanks, again."

West pulled up ten minutes later, and Astrid practically lunged at the car door. She yanked at the door handle before he unlocked it so by the time he did, it swung open hard. "Sorry, sorry."

"It's okay. You did good in there. I heard everything clearly. Let's hope Michelle heard everything clearly over the phone."

It took her three tries to snap her seat belt. When she heard the click, she said, "Let's hope Olly's okay, and that they take the bait and lead him to the falls. We don't even know if he's already shown them the card. What if they already have the card, and they did something to Olly?"

"We can't think like that. There's no reason for them to hurt Olly, once he gives them the card. As far as ID'ing them?" He lifted his shoulders. "They'll most likely be long gone off this island. I have a question for you about your meeting."

"Yeah?" She licked her lips.

"You mentioned something about Monique getting scratched by a cat, and she responded that she'd been hit with a tree branch. What did that scratch look like?"

"Pretty much like what she said. If you're not paying attention when you're hiking out here, those little branches can snap back and get you."

"It looked fresh?"

She nodded. "What are you thinking?"

"Another question." He raised one finger. "You were still wired when you were talking to Jackson. He said he overheard Monique saying that she lost something."

"That's right. I guess she was telling Michelle it wasn't her fault that she lost the memory card."

"But she didn't lose the memory card." He drummed his thumbs on the steering wheel. "They never had the memory card. They took the drone, but nobody lost that either."

"So what did she lose?"

West shot her side glance. "Olly?"

"She lost Olly?" Astrid gripped the sides of her seat with both hands, the leather slippery beneath her damp hands.

"It's just a guess. She has an injury. How'd she get it? Chasing Olly? Maybe that's why she's back in town—she lost him."

"Why hasn't he contacted me, then? Why not go back to the camp?"

"He doesn't have a phone. He's scared. He doesn't know who's out there looking for him." He brushed her cheek with his thumb. "Just a thought."

She folded her hands in her lap and squeezed so hard, her knuckles turned white. "I'm not sure this makes me feel better. If Monique lost Olly, then instead of going after him herself, she passed the duty off to someone else, probably the same person who murdered Chase and Naomi, the same person who attacked me. In other words, some vicious killer is searching for Olly, someone who chopped off a woman's finger. They may have already found him. Maybe that's the phone call Michelle was waiting for at the Crab."

"Michelle and Monique wouldn't still be in town casually sharing a drink if Olly's captor had satisfied their goal. They must still be out there, either together or separate, and hopefully Michelle's lackey is working his way to the falls right now—with or without Olly."

"And if you can corral Michelle's henchmen at the falls, we can do a proper search for Olly without worrying about the bad guys getting to him first."

"Exactly. Or they still have him, and they're marching him to Dead Falls as we speak."

Astrid grabbed his arm. "And you'll stop them, West? You'll keep them from hurting Olly?"

"I will. I swear I will, Astrid." He gritted his teeth. "Or die trying."

Astrid flickered a gaze to West's face. She'd been wrong to think that West didn't care about rescuing Olly. His life depended on it.

Chapter Nineteen

As they crossed the bridge, Dead Falls on their right, West flexed his fingers on the steering wheel and tilted his head back and forth, stretching his neck. He would be no good to Olly if his nerves got the better of him. He had to stop these people. He had to make it safe for Olly.

Astrid urged him past the regular turnout for the falls and farther up the road toward Misty Hollow. "I'll show you a place where you can park your vehicle out of sight of anyone on the road. It's a longer hike to the falls but worth it if you want to stay off the radar—and we do."

"Lead the way." He followed her directions and backed his SUV into a small outlet, where the bushes draped over the back of his vehicle. "Almost camouflaged."

Rubbing her hands together for warmth, Astrid asked, "What's the plan?"

"If we beat them here, we hide out in the caves behind the falls and wait. If they're already here, we'll draw as close as we can to figure out if Olly's with them. Then I'll handle it."

Her gaze dropped to the weapon on his hip, and she nodded. Did she trust him around her son with a gun? Now that she knew the truth about him, did she trust him around her son at all?

They stepped from the SUV and stood still, listening. The rush of the falls drowned out most sound except for the chirping of the birds that dipped in and out of the spray. West whispered, "I don't know if we could hear human voices even if they were yelling."

"Believe me, you can hear them. Doesn't mean they're not whispering like us...or searching." She crooked her finger. "Follow me."

As she pushed aside some foliage to reveal a narrow path, West crept behind her, hot on her heels. Their hiking boots, which they still wore from this morning, crunched the sticks and rocks on the ground as they traversed the rugged trail.

The steep grade of the incline had West's calves burning, but he churned his legs, determined to reach the top with Astrid...and save her son.

When they reached the ledge shelf that snaked behind the falls, Astrid scrabbled over several rocks. West took the same path, as the spray of the water coated his hair and stuck to his lashes.

Astrid seemed to disappear into the rock face until West drew level with her and saw the mouth of the cave to his left. He ducked inside and plastered himself against the rough granite wall.

A beer bottle tipped over and rolled toward the edge, and West grabbed it and pulled it back into the cave. "You'd think these kids could at least clean up after themselves."

"They usually do. We did." She squinted through the sheet of water. "Unless they come up the back way like we did, we should be able to see their approach—if they took our hint."

"So, we wait." West crouched on his haunches, resting his forearms on his thighs.

"How long should we give them?" Astrid slid down the wall of the cave and sat, knees up, with one arm wrapped around her legs.

"As long as it takes, Astrid."

She cranked her head to the side and peered into the cave. "I don't see how he could've actually buried it in the cave. It would've taken him too long to get here, bury it and then return to the campsite."

"The goons who have him don't need to know that, and if he did bury it elsewhere, he's not about to tell them now. He's been leading them on some kind of wild-goose chase. He has to be. Michelle and Monique wouldn't be hanging around Dead Falls otherwise." He reached into the pocket of his jacket and cupped a memory card in his palm.

"Where'd you get that?" Astrid poked at the object in his hand.

"I swung by the station to grab it before I went to the Salty Crab to pick you up." He juggled it in his hand. "Might as well have a decoy."

She put a finger to her lips. "Shh. I hear something."

West closed his eyes and strained his ears to pick up sound outside the rushing water, and a man's voice carried over the tops of the trees. He whispered. "They're here. Can you see anything?"

Astrid scooted closer to the cave's entrance on her knees, her hand pressed against the wall, beads of moisture sparkling in her blond hair as she poked her head outside. She held up one finger.

West asked, "One man?"

She nodded and then collapsed back inside the cave. "Olly is with him. Thank God."

West closed his hand around the memory card. "We'll lure him with this and then make a trade."

"D-do you think he'll go for it? He's not going to know if this is the card from the drone or not."

"We'll play it by ear." West swallowed. "Do you trust me?"

Her lashes fluttered. "I do."

He dug his phone out of his pocket. He had alerted his deputies to be on call for a possible incident at the falls. Now that he had his quarry in sight, he could call in the reinforcements.

He tapped his phone's display and swore. "You didn't tell me we wouldn't get service up here."

"It's spotty." She tried her own phone with no luck. "Does this mean the cavalry isn't coming? We have to do this on our own?"

"That's exactly what it means." He tensed his muscles and drew closer to the cave's entrance. "We'll wait until they climb to the end of the trail and then make our presence known. I don't want them all the way on the ledge— too many things could happen."

A steely resolve took over his body. It was the same determination he'd felt the night he went after the shooter of a toddler—before he knew that shooter was a fourteen-year-old boy. It was the same determination a cop needed to do his job to protect people. He hadn't felt it in a while.

"Come on, pick it up. That memory card had better be here, kid. I know what you've been doing—leading me around like I'm some kind of idiot. But I got inside knowledge about this place, so don't tell me you didn't leave it here. I know you did."

Olly's up-and-down adolescent voice rang out clearly. "I told you I buried it under a tree. If you'd let me keep looking at that other place, I would've found it."

West made his move when he could see both Olly and his captor clearly heading for the dangerous ledge. Bending over, he emerged from the cave, holding up the memory card. "We already found it, Olly."

The tall, muscular man hustling Olly up the trail took a step back and raised his gun. "What the hell?"

Planting his boots firmly on the ledge, West said, "We figured out where you put it, Olly. Your mom did."

Astrid popped up beside him as Olly let out a yelp. "I knew you'd left it here, Olly. You would never forget where you buried something in the woods. You were just afraid to tell me you'd been up here on your own. Isn't that right?"

West could feel the tension radiating off Astrid's body. Would Olly understand? Would he play along?

The boy let out a big sigh. "Yeah, you got me. I put it in the cave. I didn't even bury it. I was gonna take Sheriff Chandler up here this morning to show him, but that woman got me."

"What happened to her? Did she get you out of your tent and then hand you over to this man?"

"Sort of." Olly grinned. "I pushed her and got away for a bit, but this guy was waiting and grabbed me. I pretended I couldn't remember where I buried it."

The man shoved Olly, and Astrid gasped. "Shut up, kid. I knew what you were doing. I was just giving you a chance before I started *making* you tell me."

"So, whaddya say?" West waved the memory card in the air. "The card for the boy."

The man snorted and clamped one hand on the beanie covering his head. "You gotta be kidding me. I don't know what's on that card."

"And you're not going to know unless you let Olly go."

"He's our ace in the hole, Sheriff. We're not letting him go."

Astrid cried out, one arm reaching forward as if to pull her son to her chest.

"Then you're not getting the card. I'll take it back to the station, play it and find out exactly what happened to Chase Thompson."

"If that's more important to you than this boy's life, go for it." He raised his gun and leveled it at Olly's head.

Olly seemed to shrink next to his captor as West's gaze zeroed in on the man's face. Every nerve ending buzzed with adrenaline.

"If you don't hand over the card, I'll take this annoying kid with me. We'll make our getaway, regardless of what you find on the video from that drone." He shrugged one solid shoulder. "And then we'll kill him."

A strangled noise came from Astrid's throat, and she threw out an arm to brace herself.

West narrowed his eyes. "You won't get that far. Do you think we came up here alone? I have my deputies surrounding this area, ready to take you down like a dog."

"Not when I come out of here with this kid at gunpoint. These small-town hicks. They ain't got the guts, my friend. They're not going to take that risk."

From the corner of his eye, West could sense Astrid making some motions with her hands. Olly's captor hadn't noticed, all his attention on the weapon at Olly's head and West's own gun, now in his hand.

West coiled his muscles, his finger twitched on the trigger. A second later, Olly dropped to the ground, out of sight amid the foliage.

Just like he'd been trained. Just like he always would. West took the shot.

Epilogue

Olly grabbed Sherlock's scruff and wrestled the big dog to the ground. Sherlock went happily, his tongue lolling out of his mouth, his brown eyes pinned adoringly on his best friend.

When Olly poked his head up, he said, "I don't get it, Mom. Why'd you think I took the card to the caves behind the falls?"

"I wasn't absolutely sure, Olly, but since Michelle was bugging my phone, we figured we'd put it in her head that it could be there. That way, we had a meeting point. Otherwise, we didn't know where to start looking for you."

"We did hear some of the teen Scouts calling my name, but—" Olly buried his nose in Sherlock's fur "—Jerome put that gun against my head."

"I'm so sorry you had to go through that, Olly. You must've been scared."

"Scared but incredibly brave." West carried a plate of graham crackers, chocolate squares and marshmallows to the firepit. "How did you get the idea to lead Jerome around to different places to buy time?"

"Saw it in a movie once." Olly rubbed his hands together before sweeping everything he'd need for a s'more off the plate. "I hid it pretty good, didn't I? Only I'd know where to find it. What was on the memory card, anyway?"

West clicked his tongue. "I can't discuss the case, Olly."

Olly wedged his tongue in the corner of his mouth as he slid a marshmallow onto the skewer. "Did that guy… Jerome…did he die? There was a lot of blood."

West shot her a quick glance and waved at some smoke in front of his face. "Naw, but he's going to be spending a lot of time behind bars."

Astrid leveled her finger at Olly. "That is the last one, dude. You're going to get a stomachache."

"This is nothin'. You shoulda seen how many Logan and I ate at camp."

"I'm sure it was a massive amount." She reached over and ruffled his messy hair. "Don't forget, you have an appointment with Dr. Maddox tomorrow."

"I know." He squished two graham crackers together. "All we do is talk."

"It's good to talk." West twirled his own marshmallow into the fire. "I had a lot of talking appointments like that. It made me feel better about a lot of things."

"Really?" Olly's eyes grew round.

"Absolutely."

Astrid mouthed a thank-you in West's direction. She wasn't sure how much West's therapy had helped him, but shooting and killing Jerome and rescuing Olly in the process had done wonders for putting him at ease around her son.

Olly smacked his lips as he finished his gooey concoction. "Okay, I'm going to bed."

"Do you want me to tuck you in?"

"Mom!" Olly crushed his paper plate in his hand. "I can go to bed by myself."

"Okay, take Sherlock with you. He just had a bath, so he can sleep at the foot of your bed."

"Sweet!" Olly gave a short whistle, and Sherlock jumped to his feet. As Olly and Sherlock trotted up the steps, Olly called over his shoulder. "Night, Sheriff Chandler, Mom."

"Good night, Olly."

"Good night, sweetie. Leave the front door open."

When Olly disappeared into the house, Astrid dragged her chair closer to West's. "Thanks for keeping things vague for Olly. I'm not sure he needs to know a dead man dropped next to him."

"I didn't think so." West took her hand and pressed a kiss against her palm. "Thanks for trusting me with your son."

"You're his hero now. I hope you're ready for that."

"He'll get over that soon enough."

Running her thumb over his knuckles, she said, "I know you had to keep things vague for Olly, but that doesn't mean you have to keep things vague for me, too. Does it?"

"What do you mean?" His eyebrows shot up to his hairline in a manner that told her he'd been thinking of something other than the case.

"I mean—" she blew out the flaming marshmallow on the end of his skewer "—what was on that memory card? Did Olly actually capture Chase's death on the drone?"

"I can tell you. It's going to come out soon, anyway." West stretched his legs, wedging his boots against the rock encircling the firepit. "The drone *did* catch the aftermath of Chase's murder, and now it makes sense why Michelle Clark, whose real name is Claire La Croix, was so desperate to get her hands on the footage. Her daughter, Monique La Croix, is the one who shot Chase."

"Wait, wait." Astrid's hands nervously fluttered over the

flames. "I know the La Croix name. Pierre Dumas has a sister named La Croix. Dumas was the dealer my ex ratted out."

"Exactly. With Dumas in prison, his sister Claire took over the family business and brought her daughter in with her."

Astrid pressed her palms on either side of her face. "And she knew? Michelle, I mean Claire, knew who I was all that time?"

"She did, although I'm not sure she held much of a grudge against you or your ex. She liked being in control, but she didn't want to see her daughter go down for murder."

"Monique cozied up to Chase to keep an eye on him, and then discovered he was skimming. Is that what happened?"

"Pretty much, but there's more to the drone story."

"More?" She reached for the glass of wine she'd parked under her chair. "I'm gonna need another hit of this."

"Not only did the drone catch Monique with Chase's dead body on the beach, but it also showed her stashing the drugs in a cave. They did not want us to find that hideaway. So the drone gave us Chase's killer and the drop-off/pickup point the Dumas cartel was using."

"That explains a lot." She ran her nails up his muscled thigh beneath the denim of his worn jeans. "I'm just glad you were here instead of Hopkins when this all went down. The arrests of Claire and her daughter are going to put a serious damper on the drug trade on Dead Falls Island."

"Is that the only reason you're glad I'm here?" Despite West's concerted effort on his s'more, he was making a mess of it.

She sighed and slid his plate from his lap to hers. She placed the chocolate square on top of the gooey marshmallow and squished the other graham cracker on top. "Well, that and the opportunity to turn you into an out-doorsman, city boy."

"I welcome your…efforts." He plucked the treat from the plate and took a bite. "You know, I guess I have been pretty vague with you."

Her heart pounded as she watched his tongue dab at the stickiness on his lips. "I've been guilty of the same. I was afraid to tell you about Russ. Afraid to admit how gullible I was with him."

"We all make mistakes in relationships. I didn't tell you that my girlfriend in Chicago dumped me after the shooting incident, either." He shrugged and licked his fingers. "But I'm done making those mistakes, and I want to be perfectly clear with you."

"About?" She reached out and stroked a smudge of chocolate from the corner of his lip. Then she sucked the sweetness from her thumb.

He dropped his plate on the ground and pulled her into his lap. "About my feelings for you. I'm falling in love with you. Is that clear enough?"

The pounding of her heart turned into skipping as she cupped his face with one hand. "Perfectly, as long as you're okay with a mischievous boy and a mangy dog as part of the package."

"I wouldn't take that package any other way." He pressed his mouth against hers, giving her a sweet, sticky kiss to seal the deal.

As she snuggled closer against his chest, she figured she'd just have to give cops another try—at least this one.

* * * * *

*Look for the first two books in Carol Ericson's
miniseries, A Discovery Bay Novel:*

Misty Hollow Massacre
Point of Disappearance

*Both are available now wherever
Harlequin Intrigue books are sold!*